PLANK'S LAW

Lesley Choyce

PLANK'S LAW

ORCA BOOK PUBLISHERS

Library and Archives Canada Cataloguing in Publication

Choyce, Lesley, 1951-,
Plank's law / Lesley Choyce.

Issued in print and electronic formats.
ISBN 978-1-4598-1249-9 (softcover).—ISBN 978-1-4598-1250-5 (PDF).—
ISBN 978-1-4598-1251-2 (EPUB)

I. Title.
PS8555.H668P53 2017   jc813'.54   C2017-900813-7
C2017-900814-5

First published in the United States, 2017
Library of Congress Control Number: 2017932488

Summary: In this novel for teens, Trevor, who has Huntington's disease, connects
with an old man who helps him live his life more fully.

*Orca Book Publishers is dedicated to preserving the environment and has
printed this book on Forest Stewardship Council® certified paper.*

Orca Book Publishers gratefully acknowledges the support for its publishing
programs provided by the following agencies: the Government of Canada
through the Canada Book Fund and the Canada Council for the Arts,
and the Province of British Columbia through the BC Arts Council
and the Book Publishing Tax Credit.

Edited by Barbara Pulling
Cover design by Rachel Page
Cover images by Getty Images, Creative Market and Shutterstock.com.
Author photo by Nancy Snow

ORCA BOOK PUBLISHERS
www.orcabook.com

Printed and bound in Canada.

20 19 18 17 • 4 3 2 1

ALSO BY LESLEY CHOYCE

ONE

Most of my story isn't very interesting, so you'll be pleased to know I'm going to leave much of it out. I hate it when people tell you a lot of trivial things about their lives. Here's a partial list of what I will not bore you with:

1. Too many details about where I live. Let's just say it's a small town near the ocean. Small enough to know a lot of people but not everyone.

2. Why I love old, bad science-fiction movies.

3. Most of my stupid, insane dreams — especially the ones involving monsters and girls in bikinis.

4. My hopes and aspirations and especially my never-to-be-fulfilled dream of being a marine biologist.

5. My first three girlfriends — well, I thought of them as girlfriends, but they were really just friends or girls I wanted to be my girlfriend.

6. My problems, and there are several, mostly dull and obvious.

7. My philosophy of life.

8. How much money I have in the bank — all $1,278.80— saved over the course of a lifetime and mostly birthday money.

9. My family history — except perhaps the story about my grandfather, who is currently in prison for a crime he committed over a decade ago.

10. My health issues. They say I have a year to live — could be more, maybe less.

But I will begin with a rather significant event that occurred not far from my home. I had walked out of town in my new running shoes to look at the ocean. I was standing high above the sea, with a drop-off of a hundred feet or so.

Someone had purposely (or so I was told) driven their car off here not long ago, and I could still see the tire tracks in the green grass. I looked down below at the wreckage of a yellow car. Who in their right mind would buy a yellow car? I wondered. But then, this person obviously was not in their proper mind if they drove off the cliff, right?

Despite the fact that there were some really nasty rocks below that looked jagged and angry, like half-rotted teeth, I was thinking I might just leap out into the air and be able to fly. No wings, no paraglider, no parachute. Just good old-fashioned middle-of-the-night dreams of Superman flight. I was working on my courage and trying to get the right focus. I was pretty sure I could will myself to fly. There was a fine salty mist in the air that pleased me. There were some gulls catching the updraft above the wrecked yellow car. The rocks and the wreck did not scare me, since I was certain I would not end up there. I just knew I was going to fly. I could feel it in my bones.

For practice, I stepped forward, lifted my arms and then stepped back. Forward and back.

Forward and back. The gulls beneath me seemed to take the hint and flew off to the north so I wouldn't crowd them out of the sky.

My mind was in a funny place, you might say. At this point I had a 50/50 thing going. Fifty percent of me wanted to follow through, and the other fifty percent was saying I should go home and watch science-fiction movies or videos on YouTube of penguins and whales doing amazing things.

If my memory serves me well, I believe I had decided to do it. To fly.

Or take whatever punishment was due a sixteen-year-old who believed he could fly.

Step forward, arms up. Step back. (I had to stop myself from looking at the yellow car.) I was thinking about something my doctor had recently said in one of her cheery moments, lecturing me about the power of the mind over the body.

Forward, then back. I had the right rhythm, a good attitude. For all intents and purposes, I was ready to do it.

And then I heard a voice. "Go ahead, kid. Those rocks are calling out your name. I would if I was you. Why not cut to the chase and avoid all the bullshit."

I turned around and saw this old guy. This really old geezer. He had on a jacket like hunters wear, high rubber boots and a ballcap like something he might have found in the street. He didn't seem to like the way I was looking at him. "What?" he said. "You never seen an old fart like me?"

"Sorry," I said. I'm usually polite around adults. But I've been trying to change that.

"Don't be sorry. I'm ninety-three years old, if that's what you're wondering."

"I wasn't wondering."

"Of course not, chucklehead. Why would you give a rat's ass how old I am when you're about to jump off a cliff?"

"I wasn't about to jump," I said.

"Then what the fuck was that you were doing? Tai chi? Yoga?" He had a look in his eyes that told me he was probably as crazy as a rabid racoon. But that didn't scare me.

"I was just stretching," I said. How lame is that?

"Stretching, my ass. Listen, buddy, I can see why you would be wise to make the leap. I've often thought I'm making a big mistake by hanging around, busting my ass, taking shit from everyone, getting nowhere. So let's go back to the beginning of the conversation. I think you should jump. If you want some company, I'll even come along for the ride."

"I don't think you understand," I said.

"Understand? Of course I understand. You, on the other hand, don't know jack shit about anything, I can tell. How old are you anyway?"

"Sixteen."

"Six-fucking-teen," he said. "Give me a break. When I was sixteen I was raising hell. I had life by the balls." And suddenly his expression changed. "But then it all went to shit. I should have done then what you're about to do now."

I took two steps back from the edge and stared down at those tire tracks in the green grass.

"What, now you're gonna wimp out? All you kids can't commit to nothing these days. Bunch of spoiled brats."

I wasn't about to defend my generation to this old freak. But I wasn't about to let him talk me into jumping either. It's one thing to attempt unaided manned flight with the power of the mind. It's another thing to let a ninety-three-year-old grumpy geezer convince you to end your life.

"Fuck off," I said to his face.

He smiled, and I could see his teeth were bad. Like those rocks. "Now you're talking my language," he said. "Now you got my attention."

He stuck his hand out like he was going to give me a handshake. I didn't know what else to do. I reached out, took his hand. Suddenly he wrenched me toward him, wrapped his arms around me and gave me a bear hug that nearly took my breath away.

"You're gonna be all right, kid. Everything is gonna be okay."

TWO

His name was Benjamin Collier, but he said that most people — well, those few people who even talked to him — called him Plank. He couldn't remember how he got that nickname. "Kid," he said, "I've forgotten more stuff than you'll ever even know." He started walking back toward town, and I guess I just sort of followed along. Aside from almost jumping off a cliff, meeting him was about the most interesting thing that had happened to me in a long while.

"Don't think I'm gonna start unloading a whole lot of philosophical bullshit on you or anything.

Movies make it look like old people have some kind of accumulated wisdom. None of that is true. We're as confused and uncertain as young mugs like you. We've just been around long enough to know when to walk around a big pile of dog shit rather than into it."

"Sounds philosophical enough to me," I said, trying to keep up my end of the conversation.

He laughed. "Right. Guess I can't help it. When I was young, I was a teacher in high school. I taught English to young bastards like yourself."

"You don't sound like any English teacher I've ever had."

"I been out of education for a long time. I realized that I'd said everything I had to say, everything that needed to be said. Said it over and over until I got sick of it. So I quit. But that was a long time ago. Speaking of school, how come you're not in school today? It's no fucking holiday I know of."

"I don't have to go to school."

"Fuck off. What are you, some kind of genius or something?"

"No. My mom and dad let me go when I want to and not go if I want to do something else."

"Like jump off a cliff?"

"Let's just say it was a kind of experiment. A mind game."

"Bullshit. Give me the truth. If you want to hang out with Plank, you got to keep the old man entertained. I want the whole story. I was an English teacher, remember?"

So I told him what the doctors had told me. The short version.

He stopped in his tracks. "You sure you don't want to go back to the cliff? Sounds like a better deal than simply waiting for the nasty shit to hit the fan."

I shrugged. "I'm trying to figure stuff out."

"Been at that for ninety plus years, and it hasn't gotten me too far down the road to enlightenment. If I was you, I'd give up on that and, well…" He threw his hands up in the air, lost for words. "I'd just live. It's what I call Plank's Law. Stop trying to make sense of things and bloody well live your life. Really live it."

11

I guess I must have smiled right then. "That's exactly what I was thinking. But I'm not sure I know how to do it."

"Well, I've had a few clues about that, but things didn't turn out so well for me. So maybe I better keep my mouth shut. Like I said, I lectured about all I knew to students for too many years and got damn tired of hearing it. You're probably better off on your own."

"But I can't seem to get a grip on things. I *think* about doing things, but that's about it."

"Well, what kind of things do you think about doing?"

"Stupid stuff. Unimportant things. I'm smart, I know. Not a genius, but a guy with a brain."

"Brains don't count. Imagination is what counts. Part two of Plank's Law."

I tried to explain that imagination was what had me on the cliffs, but it came out all muddled.

"Look, if you're lucky enough to go to school only when you want to, then you damn well better fill your days with something that's gonna turn your crank."

Plank suddenly appeared to be very tired. "This is where I live," he said, pointing to a respectable-looking suburban house that was much like all the other houses on the street. It didn't seem to fit him at all.

"Take that look off your face. You were expecting a one-room shack or a rooming house? A crotchety old man needs his comforts. My neighbors don't like me 'cause I tell them what I think of them. So I keep to myself mostly since my wife died."

"I'm sorry."

"She was the best thing in my life. Stood by me even when I screwed up. When she left, I thought I was coming along right behind her. But that was almost twenty years ago."

"You must have really loved her."

He nodded. "Yeah. I did. It was the real thing."

"You were lucky."

"Damn straight."

"I've never really been in love," I said.

Something crept over him then. That crazy look faded. He glanced down at me with what I supposed was pity in his eyes.

"You gotta do something about that. I would if I was you."

THREE

Later that day I drew up a new list of things that I wanted to do before, well, you know. I had been putting off revising this list for a long time, maybe hoping I'd come up with something more grand.

It was a pretty lame list for a kid down to his last year on earth.

1. Get drunk.
2. Get stoned.
3. Drive a Lamborghini.
4. Get arrested.
5. Have a real girlfriend.

How mundane is that? And regarding items one through four, I really only wanted to do those things once to have the experience. I've led a sheltered life — probably because of my bad health and then the diagnosis. I was told early on I shouldn't do stuff to compromise my health. So I've always played it safe. (All except for the time I spent with Antonio when I was younger — but I'll save that for later.) It wasn't like I needed to break rules or be bad. But I wanted to step outside of the boring, sick person that was me and do things other kids were getting in trouble for.

One through three were fairly easily doable. One and two I could do any time. And I had my driver's license…my learning permit, at least. So for number three, maybe my dad, who was always beating himself up because of my condition, could figure out a way to rent a Lamborghini for a day and put me on an empty racetrack somewhere.

Getting arrested shouldn't be a big deal either. It could probably be tied in nicely with one or two, but I'd leave the Lamborghini out of it.

I wouldn't want to go to prison, like my grandfather. Just maybe experience being in jail for one night. It would cause my parents some grief, but if I explained it to my mom, she'd probably see it like cutting school and think it was okay. My mom's always been telling me to do what I want to do, not what people tell me to do. She's always said I have a good soul. She's been strong about things. My dad's gone the other way. He's a great dad, don't get me wrong, but he's had this guilt thing going. Like I said, he blames himself. The doctors say I inherited my condition from his side of the family. (But hey, I promised not to talk too much about my health. *Boring.*)

I had some other minor things that could be added to the big five:

1. Hang out with real penguins, at least for a day, and not in a zoo.

2. Follow a pod of whales in a boat for a week.

3. Fly (of course) — in some kind of glider with only the sound of the wind and no engine.

4. Star in a science-fiction movie, a big-budget one, where I get to save the earth from an asteroid or an alien invasion or out-of-control evil robots. But no vampires or zombies, please.

5. Travel to the moon and back, though this is the least likely one, given my timeline.

Even if some of these were to be doable, I'd want to do all of them *with* number five. The girlfriend thing. Which took me back to my conversation with Plank. I could still see the look of shock and then pity on his face.

I went to school the day after the cliff event and sat through my classes. Everyone pretty well ignored me. A few of my teachers had said I didn't have to do the homework, but they encouraged me to read the textbooks if I felt like it.

I said hello to three girls I thought might be potential girlfriends. I'll change their names so you won't recognize them. It went like this:

Jasmine said, "Hi, Trevor. How are you feeling?"

Paige said, "Trevor, are you okay? You don't look so good."

Kiara started to say something, but then she got a funny look on her face and walked away.

When I got home, I watched a documentary about penguins and one about whales.

That week we had Thai food at home one night and pizza three nights in a row. Fish was in there somewhere, but again, who cares what I was eating?

Along the way, I had two visits to the hospital. The first one involved blood tests. The second one involved more blood tests and a sit-down with my primary doctor, Dr. Duncan. ("Just call me Dunk.") My parents kept saying over and over that she was a really good doctor, the best, like they did before and after every visit to the hospital. There were always other teens in the room having blood tests too. Some of them were girls. Some of the girls had hair. Some didn't. Some wore scarves on their heads. Some didn't. These were, I supposed, the girls with some form of cancer. The cancer girls. For some reason, I had started thinking that girls with cancer were sexy. Once, one of them, a hairless one with no scarf, smiled at me, but it was just as the nurse was inserting the needle in me, and it hurt. I squinched up my face and then felt embarrassed, so I didn't look back at her again. Nonetheless, that smile stayed with me. It haunted me in a way I couldn't quite figure out.

I decided to visit Plank, but each time I banged on his door, no one answered. I wondered if he spent his days outside just roaming around.

The funniest thing was showing up for school and discovering it was Saturday. When I arrived and saw no one was around, I thought, This is very cool. I thought maybe I'd dropped into some alternate universe (I'm big on alternate universes) and everything was different (schools were empty, time was frozen or whatever). But the janitor, Charley Chohee, came to the door when I knocked on it. He smiled the way he always smiled. He knew about my situation — most people in the school knew about it. "Trevor, dude. It's Saturday. Go home and watch cartoons or play Ping-Pong or something. No school today."

That pretty much sums up the week, but who's keeping track of time? Not me, that's for sure. I preferred not to know which day of the week it was, which month or whatever. I didn't want to look at calendars or think about countdowns. Whenever Dr. Duncan, that most excellent of doctors whom I had nicknamed Dunkin' Donuts (but only in my head), tried to talk about how much time I might or might not have left, I would shut my ears, kind of hum inside my head and make her words go away.

On one of those days I decided not to go to school again (yes, an actual school day, possibly a Tuesday), I went looking for Plank. An old beat-up car sat in the driveway, the same one I had seen the day I first met him. He was home this time but looking a little groggy.

"I nap a lot," he grumbled. "You do that when you're fucking ninety-three years old. But since you're here, come in and have a beer. You can only have one. But we should talk."

His living room was ridiculously tidy. There were pictures of a younger Plank and his wife doing things like fishing at sea on a boat, hiking a mountain trail and getting married. He studied me as I sipped my beer and looked at the photos. The beer tasted odd — fizzy, sort of sweet but a bit sour too.

"It all seems like it was in another lifetime," he said. "But at least you lived it."

"The best parts of your life are the ones you share with someone else." He said this more like a once-upon-a-time English teacher, not like the Plank I had met on the cliff. "How have you been keeping? I was wondering if you'd made that leap yet or not."

"How come you told me go ahead and do it?" This had been bugging me. I finally had a chance to get him to explain.

"An old man has funny ideas. It was stupid of me, but I was thinking, Here's a kid who must be in serious pain to think about dashing his brains out on those rocks. Maybe he should just do it and get the job done proper."

Plank saw the puzzled look on my face. He waved his hand in the air, took a sip of his beer, then slapped himself on the forehead. "I'm not sure what got into me," he said. "But if you'd jumped, I would have probably followed your lead. Would have made a wonderful story for the papers. People would have probably imagined all kinds of crazy explanations." He picked up one of those framed photos of himself and his wife. "I've kept this place just as it was when Helen was alive. Not sure why."

"It's nice," I said.

"Nice my ass. An old man living alone in his house, dementia setting in, probably, senility, what have you. Not much of a life. Just can't seem to do anything to change it."

"What happened to Plank's Law?" I asked. "Part one."

"Oh, I still believe in it. And I'll do my damnedest to try to convince you or anyone else. It's just that when you get to be as old as I am, you like to stew in your own pity once and again."

I nodded. I understood what he was talking about, but from my perspective, it wasn't age that did it to you.

"But you," he said, shifting the subject off himself, "you find that sweetheart yet?"

I shook my head, took another sip of beer, told him about Kiara, Paige and Jasmine. "But there was a girl who smiled at me in the hospital."

"Smiled? How'd she smile?"

"She just smiled, that's all."

He set the photo back down on the table and leaned toward me as if he was ready to interrogate me. "No, idiot boy, show me how she smiled."

Before I could answer, I realized just how the image of that girl, that smile, had lingered in my mind. I had not been able to shake it.

So I tried to smile like she did but immediately realized I'd gotten it entirely wrong. "No, that's not quite it." I tried again, and then Plank's expression changed. He broke into his own broad grin.

"That's the one, lad. That's the one."

FOUR

I was diagnosed with Huntington's disease when I was ten years old. My grandfather on my father's side had it, and so did his father. My dad was spared. But not me. Up until that illuminating trip to the doctor, everyone had assumed I was simply a somewhat strange little kid — overly anxious about some things, oddly apathetic about other things. After the diagnosis I became depressed sometimes — like, really depressed if one of my favorite sci-fi TV shows was canceled or if my shoelace broke.

If I remember correctly, my parents argued a lot about whether I should be tested at all. My dad said yes. My mom said no. Mom's point was that if I had it, maybe I'd live a happier life if I didn't know. I kind of wish she had won the argument. That way I could have lived to this ripe old age of sixteen assuming I was just another anxious, somewhat apathetic, moody kid with a few aches and pains and some muscle twitches now and again.

But there it is, and while I found out that Huntington's disease, or HD, would eventually rob me of a full (if somewhat odd) life, I decided to more or less embrace my situation and think of myself as unique, although I failed to do that more often than not. (By the way, not many kids die of HD— mostly adults. Lucky me.)

When the doctor had told me what I had, she said it with a very serious voice, and I remember she had kind of a twitch in her eye. She didn't come out and tell me it would one day kill me. At that point she said she had no idea how long it would be before HD would sneak up from behind and take me down. She said I should live my life like a normal kid and wait and see. Then she suggested that my parents take me out for ice cream.

So Dad had the guilt. His genes. His fault. Once things started to make more sense (though really, how much sense can news like that make to a kid who is ten?), I figured out a few ways I could use my condition to my advantage. Mostly, this meant ice cream whenever I wanted, late nights in front of the TV watching old *Star Trek* reruns, skipping school whenever I wanted and making frequent trips to the beach to watch waves and seagulls, remaining ever hopeful I might spy penguins or whales — which is not likely to ever happen in my part of the world. I live a long, long way from Antarctica, and what whales once frequented the sea here were slaughtered by my ancestors long ago.

It had never occurred to me to try to leverage the HD card to get a girlfriend. Not until I turned sixteen and learned I was well on my way to an early grave. The girls in my life up to that point had mostly been babysitters and way too old. Some had smoked and some had used profanity, but they had all been coached to give me ice cream if I asked. Which I did often.

But before I move on, let me tell you about my mom. She is a stay-at-home mom, which is a rare thing where I live. Dad goes out and makes the money working in an office at the phone company. His job must be boring, because he never wants to talk about it. My mom had wanted a career as a dancer, but when her father (my other grandfather) was sent to prison, she went through some kind of mental thing. She was angry at her father for being so violent but also distraught that the legal system had treated him so harshly. It affected her deep down on all levels. She lost her enthusiasm for dancing and then, in some kind of weird backlash to the events, decided to have a kid herself. Which is where I came into the picture.

And now the interesting but tragic story about my grandfather. She doesn't like to talk about it, but here's what my mom said happened. Grandpop and Grandmom (although they weren't grandparents then, because I had not come along) were at home one evening listening to music and playing canasta. I believe they were drinking wine as well. All of a sudden, a business partner of my grandfather's, who was angry over something that had happened, charged into the house and threatened my grandfather. When my grandmother tried to intervene, the man knocked her down. He was a big guy with a nasty voice and a really dirty vocabulary (so the story goes). My grandfather freaked out.

Apparently, Grandpop had been working in the garden that day digging up tulip bulbs and, much to the chagrin of his wife, had left his shovel (of all things) right there in the kitchen where they were playing canasta. He was completely new to this charge-into-your-house-and-hit-the-woman scene, and I guess he did the first thing that came to his mind. He grabbed the shovel and started beating the intruder. He was really pissed off. The end result of the shovel beating was death. I'm sorry I can't make this all sound more reasonable, but read the papers sometime. Shit like this happens.

My grandfather-to-be was charged with murder. Apparently, the intruder, the business partner, was well dressed at the time of the intrusion, had no criminal record, was well liked at his Episcopal church and had a wife of his own and two kids. The prosecuting attorney made my grandfather look like a crazed canasta-playing, shovel-toting, drunk-out-of-his-mind-on-Chardonnay, cold-blooded killer. I guess it goes to show that things are not always as they appear. His lawyer had the charge reduced to manslaughter, but Grandpop was still sent to prison.

I never saw my grandfather until I was five, which was when my mom felt I was old enough to meet him face-to-face. As a kid, I sometimes daydreamed that I would grow up and become a lawyer (as well as a marine biologist) and find some legal angle to reduce my grandfather's unfairly long prison sentence. I felt in my bones that his conviction was a miscarriage of justice, and it would be up to me to extract him from prison and set him free.

My grandmother went downhill after he was put away. She got depressed, kept mostly to herself and died four years into Grandpop's sentence. If you're thinking by this point that I come from a tragic family, you aren't far off the mark.

Oddly enough, after several years the shovel was returned to my grandmother, and she gave it to my mom. I had been fascinated by that shovel ever since I'd learned the story, but it wasn't until I was ten and diagnosed with HD, lying on my bed on a sunny afternoon after nearly overdosing on ice cream, that my parents finally agreed I could keep the shovel in my bedroom. It may seem most odd, but, strangely, it cheered me up.

Along with the shovel in my bedroom, the other change after my diagnosis was that my mom thought our family should become religious. News about the imminent death of your offspring can do that. My father had been raised Catholic, but a priest had done something to him when he was young that he didn't want to talk about, so Catholicism was out. My mom had grown up without much of any religion. She started bringing home books — easy-to-read books for kids — about world religions and asked me to pick out one or two religions that interested me.

I really liked what I read about Jesus but found much about modern Christianity convoluted and confusing to my (by then) eleven-year-old brain — I had had a birthday by that time. (Yahoo! I said to myself. I made it to eleven!) The pagans had cool rituals and built interesting structures with stone, but my mom said she didn't think there were many pagans around these days. Hinduism had a lot of gods to keep track of but really great artwork, so that one was a possibility. I was surprised to find that voodooism was a religion and asked if we could learn more about it, but my dad said, "That's out of the question. There will be no voodoo in this house." He was fairly closed-minded about some things.

More books arrived from the library via my mom. I liked much of what the Muslim religion had to offer — great stuff in the afterlife — and I admired the Baha'is, the Jains and the Swedenborgians. But the Buddhists had the best ideas about death and reincarnation. If I were Hindu, I might come back as a cat or a dolphin but maybe also as a rat or spider. I was afraid of those possibilities.

I was a little kid, not a saint, and had accomplished no great good deeds. Mostly I just tried to get through the day and hoped for good science-fiction movies to watch at night. When I told my parents I wanted to be a Buddhist of some kind so I could come back as a human, maybe this time in a healthier body and a calmer state of mind, my mom asked matter-of-factly why not be a Christian (since I did like JC okay) and a Buddhist together.

"Can you be both?" I asked.

"In our house you can be whatever you want," she said.

After mulling it over, I figured that if I had a foot in both religions, when I died I'd have a choice. I could come back as a healthy kid or go to heaven. (Hell was definitely not appealing.) My mom said that the C/B thing was perfect and she'd get me some more books, and we could watch some documentaries together.

Thus, at sixteen, I had settled on those two options. The only problem was that I really wanted to stick around and see what would happen in *this* life.

And after knocking back that single beer with Plank, I kept thinking about the girl in the hospital. If she was here and now, what good would it do me to be in heaven or in some other body in a future life?

FIVE

I'm trying to explain the various forces that shaped my life, I guess, as is my style. So I think another list is in order. The basics are thus:

1. Biology — inheriting HD.
2. Parents — good, caring people with their own problems who didn't deserve a sick kid.
3. Injustice — I'm mostly thinking of my grandfather, but a lot of other things are not fair in life.
4. Attitude — I discovered early on that of my various neuroses, apathy is preferable to anxiety and depression. With apathy you can

let things wash over you and not give a shit about item three or other problems in this world, of which there are many. The big draw-back with apathy, though, is that it is addictive. If you are apathetic about too many things, you grow apathetic about everything. And that can suck.

5. Religion — Well, I did stay with the plan of reading up on Christianity and Buddhism. I became interested mostly in the founders — Jesus and Buddha. It was my dad who came up with the idea of what he called the Useful Questions. When confronted with a problem, he advised, just ask yourself, "What would Jesus do in this situation?" or "What would Buddha do?" I did find the Useful Questions worth asking when confronted with things like a bout of diar-rhea after a crappy cafeteria lunch at school or having my gym shorts pulled down by Rich Warely during a volleyball game in gym class.

6. Science-fiction movies — I've always found solace in movies in which the world is about to end

because of nuclear war, asteroids, global weather catastrophe (my personal favorite), hostile aliens who eat humans, or basic old-fashioned giant monsters. It's comforting to imagine everyone else dying along with me rather than just me dying on my own.

7. Nature — I absolutely love nature. I don't interact with it enough, but it's nice to know it's there, the whales and the penguins and even the snakes. Sometimes I can simply look at a tree or a rabbit and feel a little better.

8. The human-made world around me — Actually, I don't think the human-made world around me has shaped me much. I often don't feel like I'm part of it. The human world has given me language and cultural bias and a so-called education and lots of products to improve my life (supposedly), but aside from ice cream and the occasional decent pizza, I don't appreciate much of it.

9. Antonio Watson — He offered me what he called a "window on the world" and made life interesting.

He wasn't a savior or a saint or a founder of a world religion, but sometimes I add a variation on the Useful Questions by asking, "What would Antonio do in this situation?"

Which leads me to introduce you to my good friend who helped me get through junior high relatively unscathed by items three and eight.

Antonio hated it when anyone called him Tony, so I never called him that. Antonio (or Ant) was acceptable as long as you didn't stretch out his full name the way his mother did when she was mad at him. Sometimes he was okay being called by his last name as well.

Antonio came into my life shortly after Dr. Dunkin' Donuts pronounced that my life would be truncated (but she didn't know when). There I was, celebrating my eleventh birthday and formulating a hybrid religion, cultivating apathy over depression and basically sleepwalking through school and life. Ant arrived as a new student who had moved to town from England, of all places. And he had an accent that made him sound like he was acting in a British movie all the time. One day in class he caught me studying him. I looked away, but a few minutes later he passed me a note. The note read *How many horse's asses do you think there are in the world?*

I shrugged, but I was mildly curious. He passed me a second note. *Not sure of the exact number. But there are more horse's asses in the world than there are horses.* He nodded toward Mr. Brean, our math teacher, who was furiously writing some kind of equation on the board and talking to the blackboard rather than to the class.

I didn't think the joke was all that funny, but somehow it cheered me up. After class Antonio sidled up to me and said, "This place needs to liven up a bit, mate. What say we have a little fun?"

He nodded toward the boys' washroom, and I followed him in. "Study yourself in the mirror for a minute while I take care of some business", he said, then went into a toilet stall with his book bag. So I studied myself in the mirror like he said. I saw a person drifting through life as always and not a happy drifter at that. I heard Antonio let out a grunt, and shortly after that he opened up the stall door, smiling.

He was holding what appeared to be a brown-paper lunch bag in his hand. He held it in front of him. "Check it out."

I checked it out. There was a big turd inside. Antonio seemed pleased with himself. I thought it was disgusting, but my curiosity had definitely intensified. "C'mon," he said, inclining his head. I followed him to the school office. It was a busy place. He set the bag down on the counter without being noticed. Then, as we walked out, he called back, "someone must have left their lunch," and we left. I was unsettled and couldn't help wondering why he had drawn attention to himself like that. Why didn't he just set it down and walk away?

"The beauty of this scenario, mate, is that the deed is done and will play itself out in any number of entertaining ways," he said. "You don't have to stay around to watch the outcome. Only an egotist would feel obliged to stick around to watch the results of his own art." Yes, he used the word art.

I couldn't remember anyone in the history of my school ever doing something quite so disgusting.

And Ant had done it with such bravado. "See this look on my face?" he said. "It's called artistic satisfaction."

It turned out Antonio's father was a world-renowned physicist who moved from one university to the next, lecturing about minute obscure particles inside of atoms. Particles called pions, muons, Lambda baryons and Higgs bosons. So Ant moved around a lot too and therefore referred to his family life as Watson's Travels. While his father made a career of lecturing on the properties of the tiniest particles in existence, his son traveled the world wreaking havoc and having the time of his life.

Don't get me wrong. I thought most of Antonio's so-called "artistic achievements" were ridiculous or worse, yet I couldn't help but admire his audacity, his infectious, sarcastic humor and his inventive pranks. And he did, as he said, give me a new window on the world.

"It's about looking at an otherwise boring situation and seeing what a single person can do to elicit an assured and genuine response," he explained.

Leaving paper bags with poo in unlikely places was, of course, one of his favorite stunts. "You need to eat a lot of fiber to be at the top of your game," he admitted. He didn't like to do repeat performances at any single venue, so our school was spared after the office incident. But the dashboards of unlocked cars picked at random seemed to suit him. As did bus stations, fashionable clothing-store dressing rooms, hamburger franchises where he believed the meat had not been produced ethically, bank deposit drawers and, once, even a police station. "It's all about making a statement, flaunting commercialism and authority," he said. But he never once left a package in a post box. "Those letter carriers have it hard enough as it is," he told me. "I give 'em a break."

By the time we were twelve, Antonio was dabbling in chemistry, perhaps inspired by his father's scientific virtuosity. He started by making fart bombs out of sulfur and other chemicals. School was the obvious first target, and as soon as the bomb went off, someone pulled the fire alarm. The school emptied and fire trucks came, but, as always, Ant walked away with a smile. "No math today, chum," he chortled.

When Antonio learned of my illness, he was indignant. "Doctors. Who do they think they are? Once they give you a label, you carry it around in your head and it rules your life. I've been to shrinks — British, Canadian, American, even Australian — and they all had one label or another for me. They pin it on your shirt and expect you to walk around wearing it. Well, I burned those bloody shirts and the labels to boot. I'm a free man. That's who I am. And so should you be."

It was what my doctor would call denial, but Ant called all of it bullshit.

So this crazy Brit taught me stuff. As far as I could tell, Antonio had never actually injured anyone, but he sure annoyed a lot of people. "I offend people," he conceded. "That's what I do, and I'm proud of it. The best defense is an offense." He was always coming up with lines like that.

Ant was always urging me to "live a little," which in his mind meant causing trouble, but it just wasn't in me. I was too polite. I did enjoy observing his antics, though, and appreciated the enthusiasm he brought to each new venture. And if ever he was suspected of letting air out of car tires (all four at a time for effect) or inserting small roadkill into rolled-up newspapers on lawns, he would use his youthful British charm to talk himself out of it.

My parents liked Antonio and invited him over for dinner. He never did a dirty deed in my home. "Family is sacred," he said. "Don't ever forget that." But the smirk on his face suggested that he really meant nothing was sacred.

I was fourteen when Antonio's father got a new university lectureship in Australia. When Ant told me this, he said, "It's like a whole new canvas, a new stage. I'm going to rise to the challenge of yet another country. But I'm gonna miss you, mate. You taught me so much."

What have I *taught* you? I asked, startled. He'd been the one always trying to indoctrinate me into his ways.

Antonio looked at me long and hard. "Courage, dickhead. You're living with your inherited disease, and you're not scared. That's really something. "

And with that, my one true friend in the world was gone to the other side of the planet. Left alone with my "courage" and my loss, I settled back into the comforts of apathy and inevitability. We both had the best intentions of staying in touch, and we emailed back and forth for a bit and had a couple of Skype conversations. After a while, though, I guess we each got on with our separate lives.

Antonio's dad took another university gig after a while, and they moved on to New Zealand — even farther away. I guess Ant's antics weren't over, because I accidentally came across a story about him on the Internet. Apparently, he got himself into some really big trouble hacking computers. But he got himself out of it somehow and ended up making a pile of money. Good ol' Ant.

SIX

It wasn't until I met Plank that I realized I should have been taking Antonio's message about "living a little" more to heart long ago. I thought long and hard about what Plank had said on our last visit. Maybe the girl in the hospital was the one. It would take courage to find out. To find her. To make contact. To take my chances. I wanted to believe Watson had seen something real, something deep inside of me, some inner resource, a tiny swirling package of energy, power and will.

I asked myself all three of the Useful Questions:

1. What would Jesus do in this situation?
2. What would Buddha do?
3. What would Antonio Watson do?

Answer to one: Pray to God. Answer to two: Sit quietly and do nothing. Answer to three: No, I couldn't do that. So finally it came down to this: What would Trevor do? The old Trevor would say it would never work, whatever *it* was. He probably couldn't find that girl, he'd tell himself. He didn't even know her name. And if by some chance he did find her, she wouldn't be who he thought she was. And then, even if she was who he thought she was, she wouldn't want anything to do with Trevor Marshall.

But sitting in my quiet bedroom alone at night, Plank's words kept echoing in my head, haunting me. And I was starting to ask myself some real hard questions. *Trevor, you apathetic, pathetic, HD-stricken defeatist,* I said to myself, *you have only a year to live, maybe less. What the fuck do you want to do with that time? Eat ice cream? Watch crappy science-fiction movies? Sit on your ass and feel sorry for yourself?*

By some miracle, through that line of questioning I managed to reformulate the question. What would the new Trevor do? I asked myself, and I actually came up with some answers.

1. Spy on this girl.
2. Find out who she is.
3. Go for broke.

Item 1 would have to come first. Maybe I'd call it research instead of snooping. I'd been around hospitals much of my life. I knew blood tests were usually done in the morning, because you weren't supposed to eat before getting tested. And I was guessing the girl had cancer. She didn't have any hair, probably from chemo. Did I really want to fall in love with a sick girl, possibly a very sick girl? I stared at the dead screen of my laptop, at the ghostlike dark reflection of me. My image answered, *Yes, asshole. What do you have to lose?*

In the morning, I told my mom I wasn't going to school. I told her I was going to visit someone at the hospital instead. She looked at me oddly. "Everything okay?"

"Yes. There's just someone I met that I want to visit." I didn't mention who she was. I didn't mention a name because I didn't have one.

I arrived in the appropriate waiting room at eight thirty and waited. I watched people being summoned by nurses to go get jabbed for a blood sample. It was a fairly unhappy lot of folks, mostly older, some looking pale and sad, others trying to put a good face on it. You could tell that many of them were quite sick. Duh. This was a hospital, right? By eleven thirty, after reading *Time* and *Newsweek* and *People* and even *The National Enquirer*, I knew the girl wasn't going to show up that day. But then I realized, even a girl with cancer probably doesn't have blood work every day.

I went to the hospital cafeteria — more sick people, lots of worried-looking friends and family. I ate pizza and ice cream to steel my conviction. I walked around afterward, tray in hand, on the off chance she might be there.

Nothing.

It was time for plan B: Go up to the eighth floor

to Hematology, where cancer treatment took place, and look in every room.

I saw people walking down the hall with rolling IV bags. I heard my fair share of groaning, saw adult sons and daughters trying to cheer up sickly bedridden parents. Dare I say, it was gloomy, depressing, and made me want to get the hell out of there. The previous (more courageous and determined) me had envisioned this investigative work as exciting, exhilarating, possibly even dangerous. This was like a long bad dream. I went home empty-handed and discouraged.

But I went back the next day. And the next. Dunkin' Do had said, "Maybe a year?" That seemed impossible. I wasn't really feeling sick. But there would be a steady degeneration once it got started, she told me. Degeneration of what? Somewhere inside my body, some biological clock was ticking.

So I kept giving it one more try. Blood-test waiting room. Cancer-ward travels. Some of the patients in the beds were starting to recognize me and would give me a gingerly little wave. I waved back. One very old woman even called out to me, and I went in to her. "Water," she

said in a weak voice. "Can you give me some water?"
I took her lidded cup into the bathroom. As I filled it
from the tap, I looked in the mirror. *Don't give up*, the
guy in the mirror said. I swear I heard it out loud.

I sat with the old woman and held the cup as
she drank. She drained the cup, so I refilled it. Then
she lay back, and as her eyelids began to close, she
reached out and took my hand. I sat down beside
her and waited until she fell asleep. I thought about
Plank's story about losing his wife. I was wondering
why this woman was all alone. Maybe her family
would come later; I couldn't know. But right now she
seemed truly abandoned. It occurred to me that the
shittiest thing in the world would be to die with no
one else there. I thought about her. Then I thought
about me. Then I started thinking about the girl again.

⊟ ⊟ ⊟

At eight thirty the next morning, she was sitting in
the waiting room. I felt the blood drain out of me, felt
the loss of nerve, the realization I had created some

idiotic fantasy in my head. I understood the hopelessness of it all. I was ready to turn and run.

And then the girl looked at me, and she smiled.

There was an empty seat next to her. She tilted her head ever so slightly (or maybe I imagined it) toward the chair. My feet began to move.

I sat down — kind of like collapsed — into the vinyl seat. "Hey," I said.

"Hey. You here for more blood work?" she asked.

"Um, no. Not today."

She looked puzzled, then concerned. Something about her eyes — soft, dark, sad. "Oh," she said. I guessed the man sitting next to her was her father. He was busy tapping out a text message, but he was definitely with her. She was not alone.

A nurse walked into the room with a clipboard and looked around. She was flipping some pages and seemed a bit flustered about something. I knew that she could call out a name, the girl's name, and I'd lose my chance.

So I opened my mouth and blurted out, "I came here to find you."

"Sara Young," the nurse said. "Sara?"

The girl's father turned off his phone, tapped his daughter on the hand and began to stand up.

Sara didn't move. She was looking at me. Her father stared at me as if he thought I was a stalker.

Sara began to stand up. Then she reached for my hand. "Come with me, okay? I hate this part."

I stood up. "Sure," I said.

By now her father was giving me a distinct what-the-hell-do-you-want-with-my-daughter? vibe.

"Dad," she said, "this is…um…"

"Trevor," I said, struggling to put the two syllables together.

"Trevor," she repeated. "I met him before, here at the hospital. He's going to distract me while they put the needle in."

The father gave me the *whatever* look. And then I followed them down the hall like a lost puppy.

SEVEN

It seemed like a long walk down the hallway to that familiar, nondescript room where a dozen people sat in reclining chairs, some attended by nurses with that all-too-familiar needle. Sara was ushered to a seat with an empty chair beside it. Her father began to sit down, then looked up at me.

"I'm not getting a signal in here," he said to Sara. "You okay if I step out for a bit, or you want me to stay?" The man was a saint.

"I'm okay," she said. "You go. Trevor and I have some catching up to do."

As he walked away, I fished around in my brain, trying to find some way to start a conversation, but I'd had no practice at this and knew I was a clumsy oaf when it came to talking to girls. There was an awkward silence as she studied me. Then the all-too-efficient nurse was there. "Ready?" she said to Sara. "You know the drill."

Sara winced as the needle was inserted, never taking her eyes off me. I was convinced I had lost the ability to speak.

The needle was withdrawn.

"There," the nurse said. "Sit quietly for a few minutes, and then you can go."

Sara took a deep breath and spoke up, rescuing me from my inability to speak. "What exactly did you mean when you said you came here looking for me?"

I swallowed. "One morning a while back, in the waiting room, you smiled at me."

"I did?"

There was nothing to do but go on. "Yeah, you did. And no one has ever smiled at me like that before."

"Really?"

"Really."

"And no one ever came searching for me just because of a smile."

"I did. But how come I've never seen you before at school? I haven't been there much recently, but I'm sure I would have noticed you."

"I go to Brookfield. You know, private school princess? Uniforms and that kind of thing. But I haven't been there much recently either."

"Oh, the place where the rich kids go."

"Not all are rich, I assure you."

Another case of nerves hit me, and I didn't know what to say next. Sara took pity on me squirming in my seat. "Hey, how'd you find me anyway? Today, I mean."

"Persistence," I said. "I've been at it for about a week."

She was studying me closely, this girl with no hair, that beautiful face and those wide, soul-piercing eyes. "A week?"

"Maybe it was only five days."

"Every day?"

"Every day," I said. I couldn't read her look. Maybe now she'd see that I had been stalking her. Maybe her dad would return and she'd say, *Get me away from this creep.*

Instead she said, "That is so cute. You don't even know me."

"I'd like to change that," I blurted. My face felt suddenly hot.

Sara reached into the purse she was carrying. She took out a pen and scrap of paper, wrote a number on it and pushed it into my hand. Her touch was electric. "Why don't you call me tonight?"

Her father was walking in the door now. "Call you?" I mumbled.

"Yeah. A phone call. Like the old days."

She smiled that now-classic smile and followed her father into the hall.

I sat there stunned for a minute — maybe more. When the brisk nurse waltzed by again, she saw me sitting there. "Sonny," she said. "Your girlfriend's gone. Time to get your keister out of here. We've got other customers."

Once I'd mustered enough brain cells to find my way to the elevator and back out onto the street, I began to wonder if I had imagined the whole thing. All I had for evidence was the scrap of paper with a phone number. Maybe Sara was just trying to get rid of me, and the number she'd given me wasn't real. Why should I make a fool of myself by trying to phone?

Then I heard a clock ticking loudly in my head. It was my clock. Three hundred and sixty-five days in a year —8,760 hours, 525,600 minutes. It wasn't like I was going to drop dead exactly 500,000 minutes from now. But suddenly I had this image in my head of each and every one of those minutes. And how they could not be wasted.

I thought about dropping by school for the rest of the day. If I'd had even one friend there, I might have done just that. But Antonio was the only real friend I'd ever had, and he was long gone. School just seemed a waste of good minutes.

I headed for the sea instead, for the cliff. I stood at the edge where I had been many times before. Same sea, same gulls, same grass right up to the edge. The familiar yellow car still lay crumpled below on the rocks. There was something about that cliff edge that spoke to me about how quickly it could all be over. One minute breathing, next minute a lifeless bag of skin and broken bones, splashing blood on jagged stones.

It was a morbid reverie that I'd played a few too many times.

But today everything about this place seemed different. The salty air seemed filled with possibility.

I called Sara at 8:00 PM and got her voice mail. I hung up. If I left a message and she didn't call back, what then? I tried again at eight fifteen and again at eight thirty, each time hanging up before her voice mail kicked in. What would Buddha do? I asked myself. Be patient.

When I tried again at nine, Sara answered. "I thought you weren't going to call," she said.

"I wouldn't do that," I said. "How are you?"

"I'm good. You know, considering…"

"Yeah."

"So how do we do this?" she asked.

"Do what?" Me, ever the Dumbo.

"Get to know each other."

"I'm not good at this," I admitted. "Would you mind going first?"

"Well. Okay. I guess you can figure out that I have issues. Health issues."

"Me too."

"I've been fighting cancer for three years. It's not much fun."

"I'm sorry."

"You don't have to say that. People feeling sorry for me doesn't seem to help. I feel bad that I'm putting my dad through all this. Not much fun for him either. And I've lost most of my friends. Some I pushed away 'cause I got tired of them feeling sorry for me and bringing me down. Some dropped me right away, not wanting to be associated with a sick girl. Some stuck it out for a while but then seemed to think, *Hey, cancer for one year, okay. We're with you.*

But two years? Three? Give me a break. It's pathetic, really. Guess they think you're either supposed to croak or get cured. Doesn't always work that way, I found out."

I didn't know what to say.

"Yo. Trevor," she said, breaking the silence. "Your turn. I showed you mine, now you show me yours."

I had to laugh at that.

"Seriously. Your turn," she insisted.

"I kind of wish I didn't have to tell you the whole deal. It's kind of pathetic and boring."

"Hey, I'm the cancer girl here. You can't pull that on me. Give."

So I told her about the Huntington's disease. I hated even saying the name out loud. I hated having to explain how it is inherited, this defect in the genes, how it could kick in at any time. No cure. Just symptom treatments that only work for a while. "Only about six percent of people with HD start to go downhill before age twenty-one. From analyzing my blood, they figure I'm one of those lucky few."

All I heard was silence on the line. I swallowed hard. "You still there?" I asked.

"Yeah," she said in a whisper. "Still here. I almost said sorry right back at you. But I'm not going to." She was quiet again, and then she changed the subject. "Hey, how do you like my hair?"

"What do you mean?"

"My hair — or lack thereof. It really freaks people out. Some even think I shaved my head and that I'm, like, a punker. You wouldn't believe the looks people give me."

"How do you deal with it?"

"If I see someone staring, I give them the finger. They either get mad or they look away. Either way, point made."

"You get angry a lot?" I asked. "About the cancer?"

"Yeah, I do. You don't want to be around me then. You get angry?"

"No," I admitted. "I don't know why. I get sad, but I don't get angry."

"We gotta change that," she said. "Any plans for tomorrow?"

"Plans?"

"Are you busy going to school or getting sad or stalking other girls with cancer?"

I laughed again. "No."

"Then I have a plan."

EIGHT

Sara asked me to meet her the next day at noon at a downtown coffee shop — the Wired Monk. I'd never been there before. You might say I wasn't the coffee-shop type. Walking there, my brain was buzzing. I was nervous, yes. Excited. Afraid. Is this an actual date? I asked the sky silently. The clouds seemed indifferent. *Figure it out on your own, Trevor*, they seemed to say.

So all I could do was put one foot in front of another. I thought about Plank, who had set this thing in motion. An old geezer I hardly knew who had urged me to throw myself off a cliff but also to pursue some girl just because she had smiled at me.

The Wired Monk was crowded. People were drinking coffee and eating sandwiches, hunkered over iPads and laptops. That's the wired part, I guess. I don't know who the monk is. But no Sara was in sight. I sat down at a small round table and waited.

I watched the door as people came and went. Ten minutes passed, and still no sign of her. Maybe this was all some kind of cruel joke.

But then a stunningly beautiful girl walked in. She had long dark hair — some kind of Hollywood Cleopatra style with bangs down slightly over her eyes. I wasn't the only one in the coffee shop staring at her. The place was mostly filled with kids my age.

The girl seemed straight out of a fantasy. She surveyed the room. Then she walked directly to me, leaned over, kissed me on the forehead. "Sorry to keep you waiting," she said as she sat down.

I was speechless. This was the girl from the hospital?

"It's a wig, silly."

"Oh," I managed to say.

"You want a coffee?"

"No. Yes."

She stood up. "I'll get you something good." She walked to the counter, a move that did not go unnoticed by the other patrons. She returned with two cups of dark coffee.

"Thank you," I said.

"You're welcome. Thanks for meeting me, Trevor." She gave me a wicked grin. "Hey, watch this."

Sara tilted her head to the side, making sure the other kids in the coffee shop were watching. Of course they were. Unfolding here was *Beauty and the Geek*, and people must have been rabidly curious as to why this hottest of hot girls was with me.

That's when she slid her fingers under the wig at the front of her forehead and casually slipped it off her head. Her eyes were locked onto mine as the room went silent except for the sound of someone dropping a spoon onto the floor. She shook the wig once dramatically for effect and then set it down on the table. "There," she said. "Remember me?"

I sat there like an idiot, staring at her as she took a sip of her coffee.

"It's real hair, in case you're curious. It probably comes from India. Women grow their hair really long, cut it off and sell it. Truth is, I'm happier when I'm not wearing it. I just did that to get your attention."

"You already had my attention."

"I know. But it was fun. I like the way people react."

"Do you do that often?"

"No. I have to feel strong. It takes a kind of courage. You know, to get people looking at me and then freak them out. But I do things like that to test myself."

"Oh."

She scrunched up her face. "Trevor, if we're going to get to know each other, you're gonna have to open up."

What should I do? Was I supposed to try to impress her? I didn't have a clue. "I really like you," I said lamely.

She smiled. "I like you too. You're average."

"Oh."

She reacted to the disappointment I couldn't hide. "No, fool. Average is good. I like average."

"Okay. Average is good. I'm glad I'm average then."

"You want some more story? My story?"

"Absolutely. I bet it's not about being average though."

"It's like this. The beauty queen who walked in through the door? She was me. You start out as a pretty little baby, then a cute little girl, and then you wake up in ninth grade and discover you have boys drooling all over you. It's fun at first, but then you have to deal with those boys."

I wanted to say something but figured any syllables I could slap together would come out wrong.

She continued. "Those boys were the ones who were full of themselves, the ones who wanted arm candy. They also wanted more, of course. It was all very flattering. But it was one dead end after another. The really good-looking guys. The pretty boys. The ones with the inflated egos. The ones who were too cool to be true. They were all dead ends. Not one of them was average. That's why average — on the surface, at least — is good. I can work with that."

She was right about the average thing where I was concerned. I wasn't very proud of it though. "I think I'm tired of being average," I said. "The only thing special about me is my disease."

"Then work with that. Use it."

"I'm not sure I get what you mean," I said.

"You will. Listen, unless I put on that silly wig, guys don't look at me the way they used to. Cancer changed all that. I can't say I'm glad I got sick, but I've learned some serious shit along the way. But first tell me more about you."

"Not much to tell except about the Huntington's. Any day, I could start to go downhill — might be my mind first or my body."

"Maybe the doctors are wrong."

"No. I've done a lot of reading. It's gonna get me one way or the other."

She reached out and touched my hand. "But you're not dead yet," she said.

I smiled. "Okay, I've showed you mine, now you show me yours."

She laughed softly. "My cancer is Hodgkin's lymphoma. The chemo worked at first, and I went into remission. Then it came back, so I go in for a heavier round of chemo. Thus the bowling-ball look. And check this out."

She held out her arm, scarred in many places with needle marks. "I look like a junkie, right? And it gets worse. The chemo put me into menopause. Do you know anything about that?"

I shrugged. "Women, um, go through it when they are, like, fifty or something?"

"Yup. But not me. I'm there now. And it means I can never have kids. Bummer, huh?"

"Yeah," I said and then felt at a loss for words again. "I'm sorry."

"Sorry doesn't help, remember? Forget that. Tell me another story about you."

I took a deep breath, pulled together a handful of brain cells, realized I'd do just about anything to keep this crazy, beautiful girl sitting there talking to me. So I told her about standing on the edge of the cliff. And I told her about Plank. "He was the one who insisted I find you. And I listened."

"I'll be damned," she said. Then she lifted the wig off the table, reached over, worked it down over my head and kissed me.

NINE

When we left the coffee shop, she asked me to take her someplace that was special to me. "Don't tell me where we're going. Just take me there," she said.

So we took the bus out of town and walked to the cliff. The sun was bright, and the sea was as blue as I'd ever seen it. "It's beautiful," she said.

"Beautiful and dangerous," I said, pointing down to the yellow car below. "Just like you."

I wasn't sure why I had said that. The words just jumped out like a line from a movie.

"Dangerous? Me?"

I shrugged. I couldn't quite explain what I meant. I was in way over my head here. "What happens when this round of chemo is over?" I asked instead. "You cured then or what?"

She looked far off toward the horizon. There were a couple of ships out there, sailing off to foreign countries. "Maybe yes. Maybe no. There's still a lot of uncertainty."

"Does that part drive you crazy?" I was thinking about my own situation. "Sometimes I think the not knowing is worse than some doctor coming out and saying, *Trevor, you have* exactly 365 *days to live. Then your time's up.*"

She laughed. "It doesn't work like that. Never does. So where are you at with the whole death-and-dying thing?"

This was one serious girl. But then, hey, here we were, two potentially terminally ill teenagers standing on the edge of a cliff. Talk about your symbolism. Why wouldn't we be cutting to the chase for the big discussion about life and death?

"Well, I think I've settled for believing in reincarnation," I said. "I'm hoping to come back and start over without a disease. Kind of a second crack at it."

"As a person or an animal?"

"I don't know. I can see the advantage of both." I nodded at an osprey flying overhead carrying a fish. "That looks pretty good to me," I said. "Although I don't really like fish."

"But what about this life? You need to do something important here and now. Maybe there is no coming back. What do you want more than anything else?"

I followed that osprey with my eyes until it was lost from view. I wanted to look at Sara but didn't have the courage. As I stared off into the distance, I said, "More than anything, I want to be with you."

There's silence, and then there's silence. And then there was this. When I finally turned to look at her, everything else in the world evaporated. There was just Sara and me and empty everything else. She broke the silence that was either a few seconds or a few years long by saying, "I had you all wrong. There's nothing average about you."

❚❚❚

We were in another world, as far as I could tell. No one had ever affected me like this girl did. I'd felt nothing like this before. I had no idea where to go from here. Maybe something this amazing would just disappear. Maybe I needed to figure out a way to hang onto it. "What about you?" I asked. "The whole death-and-dying thing?"

"I'm scared," she admitted. "I try not to think about it." This seemed unlike the brazen girl who had walked into the coffee shop and yanked off her wig at our table. "I can't get a handle on the fact that when I die, when anybody dies, the world just picks up and keeps on going."

"It doesn't seem fair, does it?"

"My mom left when I was eight, and we never saw her again. My dad — you saw him — he was never the same after that. And me, well, I couldn't believe it.

It didn't seem real for a long time. Even now, I think I'll wake up in the morning and she'll still be there. I really would love to see my mother again. But it hasn't happened yet, so I guess it will never happen. It hurts so bad that I don't think the pain will ever go away. Not even when I die."

I guess she realized that last part put the focus back on me. "But let's forget about that," she said. "Let's focus on now. On us."

"Us?"

"Yeah, us."

I'd never realized before how beautiful two little letters of the alphabet could sound.

TEN

We walked along the coast for nearly two hours. I told her about my grandfather — the one who was in prison.

"When was the last time you saw him?"

"Over a year ago," I said. "He told my mom not to bring me back again. He said he didn't like me seeing him like that and I should pretend I didn't have a grandfather."

"Is he really a murderer?"

"He was convicted of manslaughter. But really, I'm pretty sure it was self-defense. This guy had been his business partner. He showed up at Grandpop's home and started threatening him. He hit my grandmother, and then my grandfather whacked him in the head with a shovel. It was a total accident that the guy died, but my grandfather was charged and convicted."

"We have to visit him. I'm starting a list," she said and took out her iPhone and punched in a note.

The sun was low in the sky now, and the sea breeze was dying down. The coppery light was illuminating her in an amazing way. She saw me looking at her, then held up her phone and took a picture of me. "Nice," was all she said. "Really nice."

"I have a list too," I told her as we walked on.

She looked like she didn't understand.

"You know? A list."

I didn't want to have to explain it, but she persisted.

"And what's on it?"

So I told her.

She stopped walking. "That's it? That's all that's on your list? Get drunk. Get stoned. Drive a fast car. Get arrested and have a girlfriend. It's kind of a short list."

"I guess I'm not that ambitious."

"So the girlfriend thing. That's just another item on your list?"

"Well, it's an important part."

I could still see she seemed a little miffed.

"What about sex?" she suddenly asked.

"What about it?"

"Have you ever had sex with someone?"

I felt embarrassed. "No," I said, and then added like a complete idiot, "the opportunity has never come up."

She couldn't help herself. She laughed. And then she saw the look on my face.

"Sorry, sorry, sorry," she said. "I just think it should be on the list." She keyed some words into her phone again. "We won't worry about the sex thing right now, okay? But you will take me to see the shovel killer, right?"

"Hey, you're talking about my grandfather."

"Sorry. I didn't mean it. But will you take me to meet him, please?"

"Sure."

"What else? Is there someone you'd really like to talk to, anyone you'd like to meet or get back together with?"

That rang a bell. "Of course," I said.

"Who?"

"Antonio Watson," I said.

"Who's that?"

So I explained about Antonio, the one of a kind. I told her about our friendship, his mentoring, his spirit. I admitted that I had been a fool, a lazy fool, for not keeping up the friendship even at long distance.

As I spoke, I thought maybe she was losing interest, because she was back to poking at her iPhone. But by the time I'd finished telling her the story of Antonio, she was holding up her phone and showing me a photo. "Bingo," she said.

I didn't recognize him at first. But then it sank in. Antonio — a little older, but Antonio for sure.

Sara pulled the phone back and scrolled down. "He lives in New Zealand?"

"The last I heard, he did. He got in trouble for hacking into some bank computers there, but somehow he only got a slap on the wrist and then got hired by one of the big banks in that country to come up with some kind of anti-hacking software."

"Really?"

"Yep. And then he sold his software and made a ton of money. I'd say my old buddy is some kind of millionaire. And he's only sixteen."

"Seventeen, actually, according to this blog I found. You really have to get in touch with your old friend."

"Put it on the list," I said.

###

A couple of days after that, I was sitting with my parents in the living room, watching *Star Trek* reruns, when I felt a wave of anxiety overtake me. And my mind just froze.

That night I felt the muscles in my face tighten in an odd way that scared me.

The next morning I went to the HD website and reread what I had read a couple of times before.

I prayed I was wrong, but maybe these were the first symptoms of the disease that was going to end my life. I didn't tell anyone. Instead, I sat in my room and watched science-fiction movies —*Total Recall, Alien, Gattica, 2001.* Sara phoned and texted a couple of times, but I told her I wasn't feeling well.

The following afternoon she showed up at my house. From my window I saw her coming up the sidewalk. She had on a different wig — one that made her look, well, normal. I listened as she talked to my mom at the front door for what seemed like an awfully long time. Then my mom yelled up, "There's someone here to see you."

I had no choice but to crawl out of my cave. I went downstairs to the living room, where my mom gave me a funny look but then quickly faded from the scene.

"Thought I better come pull you out of your gloom," Sara said.

"It's pretty gloomy. Gonna be a long haul up."

"Well, I didn't just come for you. I came for me."

"What do you mean?"

"I gotta start a new round of chemo. Even more aggressive, they say. Something that could really help. But I need a chemo buddy."

"What about your dad?"

"He'd go. But I'd rather have you."

"Not sure I'd be such good company."

"I don't care. I'm on your list, right?"

I just stared at her.

"Idiot," she said. "Having a girlfriend means you have some responsibilities."

That made me smile. For a happy, brief instant, I forgot about HD, forgot about cancer, and all I could think of was being with Sara.

"When?"

"Tomorrow," she said. "My dad will drive me there. You meet me at the hospital. It's gonna be a long day."

ELEVEN

I'd walked past that room in the hospital before. People sitting in reclining chairs, each hooked up to an intravenous drip. Toxic chemicals seeping into bodies to kill cancer cells. When I found Sara, she looked frightened.

"I can't help it," she said. "I've been through all this before. But I feel a wave of panic every time I come here. And I've never had this particular drug before. Sometimes people have bad reactions."

I held her hand. It felt warm and wonderful. A nurse guided us to Sara's chair, and she sat down.

I sat beside her on a plastic chair like the kind they have in the school cafeteria.

I tried to entertain her with a few stories about Antonio back when he was part of my life. She seemed to like it but kept drifting off. Probably from the Benadryl they gave her to keep her relaxed for the treatment. At around noon, she fell asleep. The nurse said she'd probably be out for an hour or so, and it was all perfectly normal.

"Why don't you go get some lunch," the nurse suggested.

I left, feeling a little guilty, worried that Sara might wake up and I wouldn't be there. I wasn't really hungry, but I knew I had to find out what was going on with me. I'd been in denial ever since I'd felt that first twinge a few nights back. My doctor was just downstairs on the third floor. I took the stairs instead of the elevator and asked the receptionist if I could see Dr. Duncan.

"Do you have an appointment, Trevor?"

"No. But she told me to come see her if I ever needed her. Is she in her office?"

The receptionist looked up something on a screen. "She's here, but she's on a conference call."

"Could you tell her I'm here? This is important."

She looked at me like I was asking for a big favor. I thought she was going to say no. But instead she got up, went down the hall and knocked on a door. The door opened. Dr. D., holding a phone up to her ear, listened to what she had to say, then looked in my direction.

The receptionist then came back and said, "She said she'll see you. Just go in."

My legs felt wobbly as I walked toward the office. Truth is, I didn't want to know if these were the first symptoms, if this was the beginning of the end. In fact, I wished once again that my parents had never had me tested at all. All these years, I'd had the knowledge of my illness hanging over me. Wouldn't it be better to live your life as a so-called normal person and then one day start to get sick? Wouldn't that be better than waiting for it to happen?

I tapped on the door. Dr. D. was still on the phone, but she motioned for me to come in. I sat down, and she studied my face. I didn't understand most of what she saying on the phone, but it was something medical. "Thanks for the consultation," she finally said and hung up. She turned her attention to me.

"Trevor, what brings you to this part of town?"

So I told her about my symptoms. "Is this it?" I asked. "Is this the beginning?"

Dr. Duncan shook her head. She looked gravely serious. I didn't like that. "I can't say. But let's do some more blood work. You eat anything yet this morning?"

"No." I had completely forgotten about eating breakfast in my rush to meet Sara.

"Good. I'll get a nurse to draw a sample right away. Stay put."

She left the room, and I sat there, feeling my own version of panic. I wanted to run. I truly *didn't* want to know. I didn't want to have to see the looks on my parents' faces if the news was bad. I didn't want to take a bunch of drugs for whatever symptoms must be coming. I didn't want to know that the HD would just get worse whatever treatment they gave me.

And I didn't want another prediction — this time a more dire one — about how long I had to live.

A smiling nurse arrived. "Roll up your sleeve, please."

I closed my eyes and waited for the sting of the needle. I felt total defeat. And then it was over. The needle was jabbed in, blood was drawn, and the cheerful nurse was dabbing my arm with alcohol and putting on a little round bandage. "That's it," she said. "You can go."

As I stood up, Dr. D. came back into the room. "Trevor, I'm glad you came. Go home and take it easy. I'll call you tomorrow when we know something. We'll go from there. We'll come up with a plan."

I nodded and felt dizzy as I stood. Dr. Duncan steadied me. I thought about Sara as I walked down the hall. Maybe I should call her father to come. Maybe I should just fade from the hospital and fade from her life. Going back home and crawling into bed seemed awfully tempting.

What would Jesus do?

What would Buddha do?

What would Antonio Watson do?

I knew they'd all do the same thing.

Sara was finished by three o'clock. The intravenous was removed, and the Benadryl was starting to wear off. She was wobbly on her feet, and I had to hold on to her to keep her from falling. But I was glad I had not bailed on her. I got her into a cab that was waiting in front of the hospital. I saw pity in the driver's eyes. It was the same look I'd get from people when they found out about my HD.

Her dad was waiting for us when we got to her house. He looked at me differently now. "Thanks for this, Trevor. I wanted to go myself, but Sara insisted. And when she insists…" He didn't have to finish the sentence.

I didn't want to go home right away, so I walked and walked until I found myself standing in front of the old house where Plank lived. The curtains in the windows were all shut tight. I banged on the door once, twice, three times.

"Hold your horses," I finally heard a scratchy voice calling from inside.

I waited. Then the door opened. Plank shielded his eyes from the light. He had a scruffy beard, and there was a funky smell about him. "Were you sleeping?" I asked.

"No. Just resting. Come in. This a social visit, or did you come to rob an old man?"

"You have anything worth stealing?"

"Only my dignity, and I don't think that's worth much these days. Sit," he said, motioning to an old stuffed chair.

As I settled in, I suddenly felt the events of the day sweep over me. I hit the arm of the chair with my hand. "Fuck!" I shouted. "Fuck! Fuck! Fuck!"

Plank rubbed his eyes and scratched his neck. Despite my stupid outburst, he didn't seem offended. "You came here to tell me that?"

"Sorry," I said. "Guess it needed to be said. Guess I wanted someone around to hear it."

"That's all?"

"No, there's more."

"Don't keep me in suspense. I'm old. I may not still be here by the time you finish."

I swallowed and looked at him. "Sara. Her name's Sara."

"Good name. Biblical. The wife of Abraham. If I recall correctly, she was so beautiful that Abraham was worried someone would try to steal her away from him."

"You a Christian?" I asked him.

"I was brought up in the church. Kind of got pissed off at God when my wife died. He and I haven't exactly been on speaking terms since. When she was sick, I begged God to take me instead of her, but the bugger wouldn't listen. So you can see why I'm not tight with my maker right now. Can't decide which of us should apologize first." He let out a deep sigh. "So there's this Sara girl. Tell me more."

"I spent the day in the hospital with her." I explained about the cancer and the new chemo treatments.

"That's not easy. Good man to be there for her. What else?"

So I told Plank about my symptoms.

"But you don't know yet?"

"I don't have the facts, no. But I have a feeling. This is where it begins."

Plank lowered his head and ran his fingers through his thinning gray hair. "Fuck. Fuck. Fuck," he said in a soft but angry voice. Then he looked up and said, "I think this deserves a beer."

"Two beers," I said.

"Two beers it is," Plank said as he headed for the kitchen.

TWELVE

I promised at the outset not to dwell on my health issues. I meant to stick with that, but it seems to have come up a bit more than expected. That's why I'll give you a quick and dirty summary of what Dr. D. had to tell me the next day. I went to her office with my parents. She'd said on the phone they had to be there. This was almost definitely the beginning of the "active phase" of Huntington's disease, Dr. D. confirmed. She apologized for probably having been right before about the prognosis. A year — maybe more, maybe less.

When we got home, I went back to my room and thought about Sara. I couldn't help it. I needed to make a list.

Sara was:

1. Probably the best thing that ever happened to me.
2. Beautiful — hair or no hair.
3. Full of life, spirit, personality.
4. A girl with serious health issues of her own.
5. A girl who had a good chance of kicking cancer and living a somewhat normal life.
6. A girl who shouldn't be getting into a relationship with a boy who had a year or less to live.

I started poking around the Internet for stories about people diagnosed wrongly with HD. I found a few, but that didn't cheer me up. I knew I was sick. I did a quick check of my email and discovered a message from Sara. **I found Antonio. Here's his Skype address.** She'd included a link to show me how to open a Skype account. I fooled around until I got it working, realizing the distraction, any distraction, would do me good. And once I was in, I decided that

I really did want to talk to Antonio more than just about anyone on the planet.

My first attempt failed after the little swirly picture and the sound of someone sighing. I tried again and failed. The third time, I got a voice but no image. "Yo," it said.

"Yo," I responded. "Antonio?"

"Who's this?"

"Trevor."

"Who?"

"Trevor Marshall."

And then I got a visual. It was Antonio, looking just like the photo Sara had showed me. "Holy fuck, brother. Trevor, man. I don't believe this."

I could see that he was on a beach, and it appeared to be very early morning. He must have been holding his phone in front of him. "I wanted to reconnect," I said. "How are you?"

"I'm great. Couldn't be better. Had a little grief a while back, but I'm over that."

"Yeah, I read about you."

"Some of it was true, but it wasn't the whole story. Anyway, it all turned out for the best." Antonio had that signature grin on his face. "Sorry we lost touch. I'm really bad at staying in contact. How's everything with you?"

Well, I did need to talk to someone. And I decided Antonio would be it. So I told him my latest news.

"Trevor, buddy, that is tragic. Maybe they screwed up the test. Maybe your doctor's wrong."

"I don't think so."

"What are you going to do?"

"I don't know."

Antonio looked so serious. "I'm gonna check something here. Don't go away. You'll lose me for a couple of minutes, but I'll be back."

"Sure."

I lost his image and sound but stayed put. Cutting me off seemed like a weird thing for him to do, but then, this was Antonio, the unpredictable. When he came back on he said, "I just booked myself on a flight to LA later today. I'll figure out the other connections and let you know ASAP. You still living in the same house?"

"Same house."

"Hang tight. I'll give you an update along the way."

"Are you serious? You're gonna drop everything and come visit?"

"There's nothing to drop. I'm free as a bird. Besides, I've been getting bored. You and me used to make some great stuff happen. We're getting old, and we need some time to reminisce. Stay tuned. Gotta go if I want to make that plane."

And that was that. I lost his image and sound again and sat there staring at the empty Skype screen. Then I suddenly realized I didn't feel quite so bad.

I left the house after that and went to find Sara. We sat in her backyard on a rusty metal swing set left over from when she was little. She looked pale, and I guessed it was the chemo doing nasty things to her system. She wore a scarf but no wig. I knew I had to tell her about me. So I did. I heard the defeat in my voice as I gave her the news.

Once it sank in, she had a reaction I didn't expect. She was angry. At first I thought she was going to scream at me. Then she slipped the scarf off her head and tilted her face toward the sky. She took a deep breath. "So the truth is, this isn't much different from what you already knew."

"I guess not. Just that now there are symptoms."

"Right, but you still have a choice of who you want to be in your story."

"What story?"

"The story in your head. Poor little sick boy. Or live large and die young." She still seemed angry, like she was giving me some kind of lecture.

"I'm not sure I understand."

"Are you the victim or the hero?"

I knew what I felt like. "There's no point pretending everything is going to turn out okay."

She looked deep in my eyes. "If you're a victim, then I'm a victim too. It was my decision to get involved with you. I needed you in the hospital with me to make me strong. And I need you to help me beat this thing in me. If you're feeling sorry for yourself, you won't be there to give me what I need."

"What do you need, Sara?"

"I need you, Trevor. I need you to be strong and to be there for me."

"Okay," I said. "I can do that."

"But you know what?"

"What?" I asked.

"I'm gonna be there for you too, Trevor. I promise."

THIRTEEN

I knew my doctor was obligated to tell my parents what was going on with me. I supposed they had a right to know, being my parents and all. But it didn't make things any cheerier around the house. I also knew Mom had told my grandfather, and one day after suppertime he called me on the phone, something he'd never done before. I guess hearing the news about my predicament had changed something in him and made him want to connect.

"Dammit, Trevor," my grandpop said. "I'm so sorry, son. I feel like my whole life has been stolen from me. I've never had the chance to get to know you. And now this."

"It all sucks, Grandpop. It sucks big-time. It's just not fair."

"Not much is," he said. There were a few seconds of dead air on the line, and then he added, "I know I've kept you away, but I'd really like to see you."

"You want me to visit you?"

"Yeah, if you would."

"Sure. Can I bring someone? I've got somebody I want you to meet."

"Girlfriend?"

"Yep."

"That's my boy. She got a name?"

"Sara," I said and told him all about her. Well, everything but the cancer bit.

"Gonna marry her?" It was a strange thing for him to say, but then a man who's been in prison for much of his life probably reasons that it's best to get a move on things. You never know what tomorrow will bring.

"I'm sixteen."

"In my day, sixteen was a good age to get hitched."

"I'll think about it," I said. And suddenly I had this weird urge to do it — to ask Sara. Maybe as a joke just to see what she said. I wondered if I should maybe drop the getting-arrested item on my list in favor of getting married. Poor old Grandpop.

It was great hearing his voice, but afterward, alone in my room, the insanity of everything swept over me. None of us had any real control over our lives. Shit just happened. Look at my grandfather. If Grandpop had not been gardening that day, he probably wouldn't have had the shovel handy when his pissed-off business partner showed up and started threatening him and my grandmother. But there it was. And he used it. The jury didn't see his actions as self-defense, and the judge gave him the longest sentence he could. And so it goes.

I dug a calendar out of the drawer where I'd been hiding it. When you're staring at a calendar and you have a limited amount of time to live, a lot of weird shit goes through your head. I started flipping through it. Today was May 25. The month was almost over.

June, July, August: Would it really be the last time I'd experience summer?

September: Go back to school as if everything is okay? No way.

October, November: Shorter days, less sunlight. Gloom and doom.

December: Whoopee, I get to have my last Christmas. Bet my mom and dad are gonna have a blast with that.

January and February: By that time, I might be in rough shape. Don't even want to think about it.

March: First taste of spring. Maybe I will have grown philosophical. Maybe there is a quiet wisdom that comes with dying young.

April: Gotta try to put a good face on it. Sara will be off chemo by then, I think. Getting healthy maybe. Hair growing back.

May again: I could still be here.

Or not.

I tore the fucking calendar in two and then ripped it into pieces.

My computer, which had been asleep, suddenly came back to life.

"Trevor, you there?"

I dropped down in front of the screen. Skype had kicked in. I looked into my computer camera. "Antonio. Where are ya?"

"LA. Just got in from Auckland. Man, I forgot how big the Pacific Ocean is. One more flight and I'll be there. I'll rent a car when I get in and boot it over to your place."

I noticed something strange about his neck. Some purply patch. Just the lighting maybe. I decided not to ask. "No," I said. "I'm gonna meet you at the airport."

"You sure?"

"I'm sure," I said. And he gave me the details of his flight, arriving the next morning.

"Most excellent. See you then."

And then he was gone. It was going to be great to see Antonio. He had made my life so much more interesting when he was around. What would it be like this time? Maybe I'd bounce back from my calendar crisis. Forget the months. Every day was going to have its own name. Every person I met was going to teach me something I needed to know before I hit my dead end. I felt a funny twinge in my right arm as the screen went dark. I saw my own reflection wearing a look I almost didn't recognize. Yeah, the muscles in my jaw felt tight. My mind was taking me to a dark place. I would have to fight this.

For the time being, I decided to focus on the next day. I didn't want my mom or dad to drive me to the airport. I'd need to find a car and a driver somehow. And I wanted Sara to be with me when Antonio arrived for our reunion.

FOURTEEN

I knew I was being stubborn, and probably not fair, but I didn't want my parents involved much in my current life. My dad felt guilty as always, and since the latest news from Dr. Duncan, they'd both become even more protective of me. So I didn't even tell them Antonio was on his way. I wanted a life, a truly independent life —*my* life, however long it would be. This was the new me. Mr. Independence.

But I wasn't really independent at all. None of us ever is.

Early the next morning I checked Antonio's flight to make sure it was on time, then called Sara and asked her to meet me at Plank's house. I couldn't find Plank's phone number listed anywhere, but I had a gut feeling he'd be home.

It was a funny scene. Sara arrived there before I did, and by the time I showed up, she and Plank were sitting on some old lawn furniture in the front yard. Sara had on her normal wig — the one that didn't draw much attention.

"There's the lad," I heard Plank say as I walked across the dandelions on the weedy lawn.

"I see you two have gotten to know each other," I said.

"We were just talking about you," Sara replied.

"Gossip?"

"Yep," she said.

Plank gave me a big smile and winked. But he looked tired again. "How you feeling?" I asked him.

"Old. I feel old. Ready to trade this old body in for something new. But hell, what can you do?"

"Plank, I have a favor to ask. We need a drive."
I nodded toward his car in the driveway. It was a Ford
Focus — maybe ten years old. A rust bucket. "I want to
meet a friend who's flying in."

Plank rooted around in his pocket and then
tossed me the keys.

"I don't have a license," I said. "Just a learner's
permit. And I haven't had much practice."

Plank put on his mock-mean look. "What? You
want a chauffeur as well?"

"Sort of."

"You'll owe me big-time," he huffed.

"I already owe you big-time."

"I'm keeping a tab, don't worry. One of these
days, I'm gonna call in those favors. You any good at
yard work?"

I didn't have to answer. Plank walked toward me,
grabbed his keys back and headed to his car.

Sara and I got in the back together.

"Now I really feel like a chauffeur," Plank said
with a laugh.

The inside of the car hadn't been cleaned in a long time. There were McDonald's wrappers, newspapers, some dirty socks. It smelled faintly of urine.

"Nice ride," I said, trying to sound sarcastic and funny at once.

We pulled out of the driveway and onto the street.

"Bought this brand-new. Still seems like a new car to me. Helen and I drove it across the country once. Lot of memories in this old heap. My eyesight isn't that good, by the way, so feel free to pipe up if you see a dump truck headed our way or a cop on the horizon. Don't want another speeding ticket."

Once we got out on the highway, Plank was driving so slow that cars were backed up behind us. A couple of drivers hit their horns. Plank looked in the rearview mirror and then rolled his window down and put his left arm out. He held it high in the air, middle finger pointing at the sky. Sara laughed.

"Lack of respect for their elders," Plank said. "It's not like the old days."

At the airport, Plank pulled up to the curb at the arrivals door. "I'll stay here. I need a nap. You two go get your friend. What the hell did you say his name was? Alonzo?"

"Antonio," I said.

"Ah, like Vivaldi?" Plank said.

"Who?" I asked.

"Antonio Lucio Vivaldi. The baroque composer. Helen used to love to listen to his music."

Inside the airport, I checked the board to see if Antonio's plane had landed. People hurried past us as we tried to get our bearings. I started in the direction of the luggage carousel, but Sara grabbed my hand and stopped me.

"Hey, Trevor. What if we could get on one of those planes? Just you and me, and fly off somewhere?" She nodded to the departures board. "Pick one."

I looked at the list of planes departing. Toronto. Philadelphia. London. Paris. Miami. Cleveland.

"Cleveland," I said.

"Idiot. Why Cleveland?"

"'Cause it wouldn't matter where we went. If I was with you, I'd be happy to be anywhere. Even Cleveland."

She smiled. Her smile, her eyes, her presence made me dizzy. And then she pulled me to her and kissed me. Right there in the middle of the busy airport crowd.

"Wherever that was," I said, "it was better than London or Paris. Even better than Cleveland."

By that point I'd almost forgotten about Antonio. Sara had taken me into a dream world. As I tried to get my focus back, I saw him. He was standing at an airline counter, arguing with an agent. His voice was loud and his attitude aggressive.

I led Sara over to him and watched as the airline agent, a young guy with an immaculate haircut, nodded and listened to Antonio's ranting. "You lost my freaking suitcase, so what am I supposed to do?" he shouted.

I tapped him lightly on the shoulder. He spun around. As he realized who I was, the hostility seemed to drain out of him. "Trevor, my man. You came to my rescue." Then he abruptly turned back to the airline agent. "Just forget it," he said. "I didn't need any of the shit in there anyway." As he turned back to me, I spotted what I had seen on Skype. Something on his neck.

He noticed me looking. "A Maori tattoo. Supposed to bring good luck and protection."

"You always seemed to have good luck. What do you need protection from?"

"Airlines. And evil spirits. And boring people. Those are the top three."

"This is Sara," I said, a bit slow on the introduction.

"You guys look great together. When's the wedding?"

I knew he was being sarcastic, but it seemed like an odd coincidence for him to say that.

Sara looked him in the eye and said, "Next week. Apparently, you're gonna be best man."

"Sweet," Antonio said and gave her a big hug.

As we walked outside and I pointed to Plank's rustmobile, this vision swept over me. I don't know why. But in my mind I saw Sara and me, older, maybe in our twenties, standing before a minister in a summer garden. I'd never envisioned myself getting married until now. It was as weird as weird could be.

I ushered Antonio into the front seat of the car. When Plank opened his eyes, he didn't seem to know where he was at first. Antonio, by way of introduction, launched into a story about his flight from Auckland and his lost luggage, followed by a brief description of his hacking career, exoneration and short but grand road to wealth.

"Holy shit," Plank said in response to Antonio's story. Once again I noticed that Plank didn't look all that well.

A traffic cop was tapping on the driver's window now. "You can't stay here, Grandpa," the cop said. "Gotta move on."

Plank nodded, but Antonio was already opening his door and getting out. He walked around the car and started lecturing the traffic cop. I couldn't hear all of what he had to say, but there was a lot of finger pointing and that same aggressive language I'd heard at the airline counter. In the end, the cop waved his hands in the air and walked away. Typical Antonio. Nothing had changed. He was like Teflon. He'd cause all kinds of trouble, but it would slide off him. He could get away with anything.

Antonio got back in the car. "Sometimes the uniform goes to their head," he said. "I think that went well though." He seemed quite satisfied with himself.

Plank let out a sigh and rubbed his forehead. "Sorry, kids. I don't know what's wrong with me, but I'm not sure I should be driving right now. That little nap left me feeling groggy."

"I'll drive," Antonio offered. "No problemo."

"You drive back in New Zealand?"

"Hell yeah. One of my hobbies is race cars. Porsches, Maseratis, that sort of thing. I've spent a fair amount of time on the tracks."

I was suddenly jealous of him. "Bullshit," I said.

"No bullshit. I took lessons. I competed. Had a couple of close calls but nothing I couldn't walk away from."

Antonio got out of the passenger side and walked around the car as Plank slid across the front seat.

Antonio plunked himself down in the driver's seat, adjusted the mirror and fixed on something. I turned around and saw the traffic cop coming back our way.

"Buckle up, kiddies," Antonio said, although he didn't have his own seat belt on. And then he started the engine and floored it, tires squealing as we pulled out into the traffic.

Plank leaned against the window and started to doze.

Sara leaned forward. "You all right, Plank?" she asked.

"Just taking a little snooze," he said. "Don't worry about me."

Antonio drove like a madman on the highway. It was like a scene from a car chase in a Hollywood movie as he passed one car after another — first right and then left. "In New Zealand they drive on the left side of the road," he said. "So this is a tad confusing. But I think I'm getting the hang of it."

"Antonio," I said. "You ever drive a Lamborghini?"

"Only once," he said. "But it was a blast."

FIFTEEN

Plank woke up as we came to a bumpy stop in his driveway.

"Driving around this old town brings back memories," Antonio said. "You and me, Trev — remember all the good times we had?"

"Sure."

Antonio looked antsy. "I can't really believe I'm here," he said. "But right now, I'm feeling the jet lag kick in." He fiddled with his phone until he found what he wanted, called for a cab and hung up.

"You didn't need to do that. You can stay at my house," I said. "It's a short walk."

"Nope, little brother. Gonna stay at a hotel. Don't want to intrude. We'll have a serious mano-a-mano session after I get some sleep." He popped a pill and swallowed hard. "We have a lot to catch up on. But later."

Sara walked Plank into the house. The two of them had really hit it off. There was an awkward silence in the car as we waited for Antonio's taxi. "You really dying, Trevor?"

"That's what they say."

"You don't look sick."

"I know."

"What are you going to do about it?"

"I don't know. I'm working on that. Trying to remain faithful to Plank's Law, part one."

"What the hell is that?"

"Plank says I should stop trying to figure things out and just live."

"Who is that old guy anyway?" Antonio asked.

I smiled and didn't quite know how to explain about Plank. "He's my spiritual advisor," I said, and Antonio laughed.

Sara was coming out of the house. I opened the car door and stepped out. I didn't want her to be in on this conversation. Antonio got out too and stretched his arms like a cat. "Jet lag. It's killin' me."

The cab arrived and Antonio got in. "Ciao, brother and sister. Catch you later, Trev."

Sara and I sat down on Plank's old lawn furniture. "Plank okay?" I asked her.

"I don't know. I took him to his bedroom, and he just lay down on top of his bed. I put a cover over him and he said, 'Thanks, darlin'.' Then he said a name."

"Helen?"

"I think so."

"His wife. The one in all the pictures."

"Must be hell to lose someone you really love," she said. I felt the muscles in my neck tighten, and I thought I felt a headache coming on.

"There's something not quite right with Antonio," she said after a long silence. I'd had the same feeling, though I couldn't quite nail it down.

"He had a long flight," I said. "Maybe it's the jet lag. And besides, he was always wired for trouble. Brilliant people like Antonio charge like bulls through the world." Back in the day, I had admired him for that. I'd wanted to be more like him.

"Why do you think he came all this way to see you?"

"I guess he feels sorry for me. I told him about the diagnosis."

Sara slowly peeled off her wig. "Do you mind? It's kinda itchy."

"No, I don't mind."

She seemed self-conscious, and I wasn't sure why — she'd taken off her other wig in the coffeehouse and enjoyed the attention it brought. Then her look turned to something else.

"My doctor was wrong," she said shyly.

"Wrong about what, the cancer?" I didn't like the way this conversation was going. I was sure she was about to say something really terrible.

"Not that. About menopause. I got my period."

"You did?"

"It means that part of me is still working. It means I could still get pregnant."

I sat silently taking this in. I remembered my silly fleeting vision of the garden wedding for Sara and me. It was a scene I knew would never happen. And then I thought about Sara after I was gone. I knew in my heart she was going to get better. The chemo would work this time. I saw her far in the future — an adult woman. A happy woman with a real life.

"This is great news," I said.

"I've been doing a lot of thinking about it. And about you. I was thinking about your list."

"What does my list have to do with it?"

"I have a new list."

"But you don't need one."

"But it's still my list. It's short."

"How short?"

"Short short."

I said nothing.

"Wanna hear it?"

"Sure."

"I want a boyfriend, a really kind, loving boyfriend."

"Guess you better start looking," I said, trying to lighten things up.

"Jerk." She smiled. "I already checked that one off. Wanna hear what else?"

"Maybe."

"I want him to make love to me."

"Have sex?"

"Yes."

"I'm not sure. I'm kind of shy in that department." Now the conversation was making me uncomfortable. I thought I'd steered us away from that before.

"There's more. But you have to promise not to say one word. Not right away. Otherwise I'll start crying. And you don't want me crying, believe me."

"No, I don't want you crying."

"I want you to make love to me, and I want to get pregnant. I want to have a baby."

My mind froze. No way had I seen that coming. Sara knew what I knew about Huntington's. My own parents had wrestled with whether it was right to gamble and have a child. Someone carrying HD has a 50 percent chance of passing it on. Sara knew this. We'd talked about it.

"I know what you're thinking," she said. "But even if the baby —"

I didn't wait for her to finish the sentence. I had to speak. "Even if the baby had Huntington's," I said way too loudly, "you'd still want to have it?"

"Yes," she said emphatically. "I would."

SIXTEEN

I can't fully describe the mix of emotions I was feeling. As I walked Sara home, we didn't say more than five words. When we got to her house, she kissed me on the cheek. "Just think about it," she said. "It's not as crazy as it sounds. Look at you. If your parents had decided not to have a baby, you would never have come into the world. And I would never have gotten to know you. Maybe it doesn't matter how long a life is as long as you live it to the fullest."

As I continued on to my own house, my legs felt stiff, making me think I was walking kind of funny.

It could have been my imagination, or it could have been some early symptoms. I'd read about the signs: stiffness, mood swings, a gradual loss of coordination. Mental decline into a kind of dementia. It was too depressing to even think about. But Sara was right about one thing — living life to the fullest. All I needed was the courage to do just that.

▯ ▯ ▯

My parents were surprised to hear that Antonio was back in town. But they had an appointment with a lawyer first thing the next morning and were gone when I awoke to the sound of a car squealing to a stop in the driveway. I jumped out of bed, and there was Antonio, in what looked to be a brand-new Porsche convertible. I could see he had gotten his spark back as he hopped out of the car and quickly crossed the lawn. The doorbell rang. I threw on some clothes, then raced downstairs to greet him, almost tripping over my feet.

"Check it out," he said, pointing to the car. "It's a 911."

"You rented it."

"I bought it. This morning."

"You planning a road trip or something?"

"It's not for me, bucko. It's for you." He held out the keys.

I was dumbfounded. "A joke, right?"

"No joke."

My brain was still in a morning fog. I found myself thinking about my list. The Lamborghini. I'd never mentioned my list or the car to Antonio. This was no Lamborghini. But it was close enough. "I can't drive a standard."

"Don't worry. I got you an automatic. The car salesman almost started crying when I asked for a 911 with an automatic tranny. Hop in. Let's take it for a spin."

I'd learned long ago that Antonio had his own rules, and there was no point trying to play by any other set of standards.

I was nervous, so I did a bad job of backing out of the driveway — over the grass and sidewalk and down over the curb. But going forward was much easier.

Antonio coached me — no jokes, no hype. "Take 'er slow and easy. Watch the other drivers, but don't let them razz you or make you do anything you don't want to do." I was a little jerky with the gas and a bit too heavy when it came time to brake, but I began to feel the car respond to my hands and feet, and it felt good.

We drove by the old school we had gone to what seemed like a lifetime ago. "Fond memories or what?" Antonio asked.

"Things were never quite the same after you left."

"I wish I could have stayed. For the first few years in Australia and New Zealand, I felt totally disconnected. And my dad moved us from one place to another. I could never get my feet on the ground. How come you and I lost contact with each other?"

"I don't know," I said. "It's just what people do. We move on." But as soon as I said it, I wasn't thinking about him. I was thinking about me. In the not-too-distant future I'd be gone, and, like it or not, everyone else would get on with their lives and forget me.

"Let's go to the beach," Antonio said.

"Sure." I took the road out of town toward the ocean, driving by the cliff where I'd met Plank. Farther on I pulled into a parking lot near the sand dunes. We didn't go unnoticed by a couple of girls sipping coffee in their car. This was just like Antonio. Whatever he did, all eyes were on him. But this time I was part of the package.

"This car's a babe magnet, dude," he said. "You'll have to learn how to defend yourself."

I laughed. We got out and went walking on the beach. The sun was bright, and there was a light breeze off the land, making the green-blue waves steep and beautiful to look at. I told him about Sara, about what she had proposed.

"What are you going to do?" he asked.

"I'm not going to let her have a kid with HD."

"You don't know for sure the disease would be passed on."

"If not to this kid, then it would show up somewhere down the line."

"But by then, there might be a cure."

"No. I can't take the chance."

"Okay, Mr. Ethical, I guess you know what you're doing. But I'm jealous. I really am. You have it all. I wish I had what you have."

I stopped in my tracks. "What are you, totally out of your mind?" Here was Antonio — brilliant, rich, healthy, free to do anything with his life — envying me?

"Trevor, let me ask you this, point blank. Aside from the Huntington's, are you happy?"

"How can I be happy? I'm dying," I snapped.

"Yeah yeah. Blah, blah, blah. We all know that. But you don't look like you're dying. You seem healthy to me, and you're not dead yet. You have this girl who really digs you. You live here in the town where you grew up, a place that feels like home to you. You have two parents who are really good to you. You've got a lot to live for."

I stopped and looked far out to sea and shook my head. I couldn't bring myself to say it out loud, but…yeah, aside from my disease, ignoring that I was worried about Sara and her cancer, and ruling out the background sadness of knowing my grandpop was wrongly in prison and…well, yes, I was probably happier than I'd ever been. I guess I must have let myself smile just then.

"See?" Antonio said, smacking me on the shoulder. "I knew it."

"But it won't last. It can't last," I added, wishing of course that it could.

Antonio was animated now. "Nothing ever does, Trev. But I'm glad for you. Stay with the program — whatever the hell your program is. Stick with the old fart's advice. What was it? Plank's Law. C'mon, you seem to have things figured out a whole lot better than me."

"No way. You were always the one making up your own rules and in control."

"Nah. That was all bullshit. I'm fucked. I got nothing. No girl who loves me, no real home, no anchors. I don't even know what I believe in."

"You're saying you're not happy?"

"Exactly. I have money. I don't need to work. I've done all kinds of things that should have been fun or meaningful. But I don't get up in the morning with any direction or purpose. I'm lost, Trevor ol' buddy. That's partly why I came to see you."

"I don't get it."

"I'm depressed. I've been depressed for quite a while. Can't seem to kick it. I thought you might be able to help."

"How?"

"I don't know. Teach me how to be like you."

By midafternoon Antonio was fading again from jet lag, so I drove him back to the Poseidon Hotel, the fanciest hotel in town. At his insistence, I kept the car. "You learned quick, kid. Just remember to keep an eye in your rearview mirror. There are a lot of assholes on the road."

I called Sara and told her I was coming by to pick her up.

"Pick me up?" she asked.

"You'll see," I said.

SEVENTEEN

I didn't have a proper license, of course, and wondered what would happen if I got stopped. I knew I was pretty conspicuous in the Porsche. But I sloughed it off. What was the worst that could happen? I'd be arrested. Wasn't that on my list?

Still, I kept my driving low-key and obeyed every speed limit, light and stop sign. I passed at least two police cruisers. No problem.

Sara came out of her house as I pulled up along the curb out front. She had on her Cleopatra wig.

Her eyes were wide as she approached. I tilted my head back with a wide grin on my face.

"Did you steal this?" she asked.

"It was a gift," I said. "Get in."

As we drove around, I told her about my morning, but I didn't tell her that I had talked about the sex and baby thing with Antonio.

"He's right, you know," she said. "About you. Aside from obvious worries, you are in a good place."

"But what I want more than anything in the world is for *you* to get better. When is your next round of chemo?"

"Next week."

"I want to be there with you."

She smiled and leaned over and put her hand on my shoulder. It sent an electric shock running through my body.

We stayed quiet for a while after that, and I began to think about Plank. He hadn't looked so good the day before, but because of the Porsche thing today, I'd forgotten all about him. "Let's go check on Plank," I said.

I pulled in behind Plank's old Ford. Sara and I knocked on his door. There was no answer. I tried again. Still no answer. I tried the handle. It wasn't locked, so we went in. All the lights were on, but there was no sign of the old guy. I called out his name but didn't get an answer, so we headed for the bedroom.

Plank was dressed, lying on top of his bed, his hand over his chest. Sara leaned over his face. "He's breathing," she said. "But it sounds funny."

Plank's mouth was open, and his face was pale with beads of sweat. "Plank!" I shouted.

His eyes opened, and his eyelids fluttered. I saw the same confusion I'd noticed the day before. I leaned over so he could see my face. "Tell us what's wrong," I said.

He was having trouble speaking. "I don't know," he said in a feeble voice. "I was feeling tired and a little dizzy. Having a hard time seeing…" His voice trailed off as he closed his eyes again.

I looked at Sara. "We gotta do something."

"We should call for an ambulance," Sara said.

"Hospital's only a couple of blocks away. I don't want to wait for an ambulance. Let's take him to emergency."

Sara agreed. Plank was a scrawny old guy who didn't weigh much, but we had a hard time getting him to the Porsche and inside. Sara sat with him in the passenger seat, holding him upright. I blew the car horn as we pulled up to the emergency entrance at the hospital. Two orderlies rushed out. One grabbed an empty wheelchair, and they wheeled Plank inside. Sara and I were ushered into a waiting room, and we sat there staring at each other.

"Seems like we keep ending up here," she said.

Her words resonated in some profound and frightening way. My doctor visits, her treatment, now Plank. But my thoughts ran to the future — more chemo for Sara, more what for me? And my final days. Would they be spent here as well? Sara saw the look on my face and squeezed my hand. I think she was reading my mind.

We waited for over an hour, and then I went up to the desk and started asking questions.

"Are you family?" a nurse asked.

"Yes," I answered without hesitation.

The nurse looked uncertain, but she pulled out a chart and then nodded. "This way."

We followed her to a curtained section of the emergency room. Plank was sitting up in bed with an oxygen mask on. He waved a hand as we walked in with a doctor right on our heels. The doctor might have been a resident. He looked really young.

"He's had a transient ischemic attack," the young doctor said, "what most people call a mini-stroke. He's stable now and should be okay, but he'll need to stay on medication. We'll keep an eye on him, and if all goes well, he should be able to go home in a few days." The doctor looked at Sara and then me, checked his watch and said, "Any questions?"

"Is he really gonna be okay?" I asked.

The doctor smiled. "I think so," he said. "But keep in mind, he's over ninety. What can I say?" And then he left.

Plank was more alert now. He was fumbling with his oxygen mask, and when he got it off, I could see there was a spark in his eyes. "That a real doctor or just someone pretending?" he asked. "He didn't look old enough to be out of high school. Hear the way he said that? Over ninety, my ass. Smart-aleck little bastard. I'll show him."

EIGHTEEN

Plank was released from the hospital a few days later. When Sara and I visited with him at home, he seemed more or less the same as before his mini-stroke. "The bastards in the hospital don't know their asses from their elbows. It's good to be home."

My parents thought that the Porsche — and me driving it — was a bad idea. They gave me a big lecture about the dangers of someone my age driving a fast car. And they let me know they thought Antonio was irresponsible for giving it to me. I listened dutifully to what they had to say and didn't put up an argument.

They usually ended up letting me get away with things they didn't exactly approve of. Out of respect for my parents, though, I told Antonio to keep the car at the hotel and I'd use it when I wanted to.

Antonio said he was cool with that. And it turned out he liked taking the Porsche for long drives. "It gets my mind off things," he said in a vague sort of way when I dropped by his room at the hotel. I tried to get him to explain what he meant.

"Some people were just not meant to be happy, Trev," he told me, "and I happen to be one of those people."

I wanted to shake him or hit him or something. "Antonio, that doesn't make any sense." I wanted to give him a list of why he should be happy. It was a long list. But I knew a lecture wouldn't do any good.

Antonio kept right on. "I've been an asshole to people most of my life, and I can't seem to change the way I operate. But here's the deal."

"What deal?"

"I'm turning all my good luck over to you. And my power. From now on, they're yours."

"That's bullshit," I said.

"Maybe it is. Maybe it isn't," Antonio shot back. "Let's drive to the beach, big boy."

But it was Monday morning. Another hospital day. "I can't. I need to take Sara to the hospital for chemo."

Antonio picked up the car keys. "I'll drive you then."

We drove to Sara's house and then to the hospital. Antonio chattered the whole way — a kind of rant about all the things wrong in the world. It seemed he had an opinion about everything. He was acting antsy again, not exactly what Sara needed before starting her new treatment. But as he dropped us off, he seemed to calm down a little.

"Sara, you take care of this guy," he said to her. It seemed an odd thing to blurt out, considering the circumstances. He looked at me. "Remember. Luck and power." And then he sped off out of the hospital parking lot.

▉ ▉ ▉

Sara had several day-long sessions of chemo that week, and I sat with her each time. I read to her sometimes or just held her hand as she got drowsy and slipped off to sleep. The doctor and nurses were kind to her, but it was a rough week, and the cancer drugs fed in through the tubes were wearing her down.

Her father stopped in at the hospital at least once a day. He offered to stay, but each time Sara shook her head. "I've got Trevor to take care of me," she said.

On Friday, Sara was asleep when her dad arrived. "Her doctor says he'd like her to stay in the hospital so they can keep an eye on her," he told me.

"Sara and I already talked about that," I said. "She's against it. She says she'd really hate it."

"I don't know," he said. "This has been a bad week. The toughest yet." We'd both watched Sara get weaker and grow more pale.

"But she's done with this round of treatment now."

He nodded. "I'll watch her over the weekend and see." And he reached into his wallet and gave me money to take Sara home in a taxi. He had a sad, defeated look about him, another parent feeling guilty that he couldn't save his kid from pain and suffering.

At the end of the day I took Sara home and sat with her in her bedroom as she fell asleep. She was as bad as I'd ever seen her, but I refused to get pessimistic. The doctor and nurses had all said that her reaction was normal. The doc wasn't sure if the chemo drugs were working yet though. It would take time to determine that.

When I got downstairs, Sara's dad was in the kitchen. I sat down across the table from him. "You think she's gonna get better?" he asked, as if I had some secret knowledge that no one else had.

He had that agonized-parent look my own dad had sometimes. I didn't say anything at first. His question hinted at the possibility that she would not get better, that the cancer would eventually destroy her. But all week, sitting quietly with her in the treatment room, I'd had this feeling. Despite the bleak surroundings and the sadness of a room filled with cancer patients, despite my knowledge of my own fate, this feeling had been building. Totally irrational, but there it was. I felt lucky to have Sara. I felt lucky to be alive. And I was beginning to believe I had some new kind of inner strength. I couldn't explain why, but for once I didn't fear the future — any part of it.

"I do," I finally said. "She will get better. I'm sure of it." And I don't think I had ever been more certain of anything in my life.

Her dad wiped a tear away and gave me a half-hearted smile. "Thanks for that. And what about you? How are you doing?"

Sara's dad knew all about my condition. Hell, everyone knew about my condition. People had been feeling sorry for me for years. I wished I could tell each and every one of them not to. "I'm good," I said. "I'm really good." There was truth in that. My concentration on Sara's well-being had made me stop worrying about myself. I might have been ignoring those symptoms I was having, or maybe I wasn't having them at all.

"Just keep doing what you're doing for Sara, okay?" He was looking me in the eye now.

"I will. I promise."

It was really strange, but I hadn't heard from Antonio all week. I'd been leaving messages on his cell, but he never phoned back. I wondered if he had left town on an impulse and flown off someplace else, but the woman who answered the phone at the hotel said he was still checked in.

After leaving Sara's house that evening, I stopped by to visit Plank.

"I'm fine," he assured me. "Totally fine. Those idiots at the hospital don't know what they're talking about. Mini-stroke, my ass. I was just tired was all. They wanted to do more tests, but I told them to bugger off. Then they sent around a friggin' nurse to check me out. She came to the house and gave me a snooty look, said she didn't like my housekeeping and I wasn't taking proper care of myself. She suggested I needed someone to live with me, so I asked her to bring my wife back from the dead. That kind of stopped her in her tracks. Who'd want to live with an old fart like me anyway?"

Plank was definitely back up to speed. I wished him well and headed home.

The next morning, my mom got a call from Grandpop. I watched as she listened and her face lit up into a smile. She put her hand over the phone and said to my dad, "He had a parole hearing yesterday. They're going to let him out."

She was doing a little dance around the room. I'd never seen her so happy. Then she was thrusting the phone at me. "He wants to talk to you, Trevor."

"Hello," I said.

"Trevor, guess your mom told you. Four weeks, and then I'm out."

"That's great. How'd it happen?"

The line was strangely silent for a minute. "I'll tell you when you come visit. I know I've kept you at a distance — it all seemed so hopeless. I didn't want to muck up your life any more than I already had. But now it's different. And I don't want to wait four more weeks to see my grandson. Promise me you'll come as soon as you can. And bring your girlfriend.

That is, as long as she's okay with knowing you're related to a hardened criminal. Wednesday afternoon is visiting day."

"We'll be there Wednesday," I said. I wasn't sure if Sara would be well enough, but there was no chemo scheduled for the upcoming week, and I really wanted her along.

NINETEEN

Grandpop had said to come without my mom and dad because he wanted to tell me something in private. That suited me. I was still on this kick of being Mr. Independence. And liking it.

I phoned Antonio, and he answered this time. "Why haven't you returned my calls?" I asked.

"Sorry, dude. Something about being back here has really freaked me out. I don't know what it is, but I feel like I should have stayed here. I'm pissed that my father moved us so many times I never got a chance to feel like anyplace was my real home."

"Well, you're here now, so enjoy it."

"Yeah, I wish I could." His voice sounded strange, not like the old Ant at all. "It's like I don't fit in anywhere. Like I don't have any real family or friends."

"I'm your friend, asshole," I chided him.

"I know," he said, but he still seemed down.

I told him about my grandfather and asked him if I could use the car to go visit him.

"Of course," he said. "It's yours. I bought it for you. I'm sorry I've been hogging it. It's just that those long drives make me feel a bit better. But don't worry. I'm going to split soon."

"You're leaving?"

"Yeah, I'll be fine once I move out of this crappy hotel," he said. "I've been thinking about this new project I want to work on. Trouble is, I have to fly halfway across the world again to get it going. That's the way I am though. If I get something stuck in my head, I just gotta do it."

I didn't know what to say to that, or exactly what to make of Antonio.

"How's Sara doing?" he asked, changing the subject. "I knew you guys had a big week, so I didn't want to be in the way."

"She's doing okay. But listen, let's get together before you leave and relive those old times."

"Sure thing, cowboy. And hey, I'm really glad about your grandfather getting released. I'll leave the car keys at the front desk in case I'm not here when you show up."

I drove cautiously after I picked up the Porsche on Wednesday. There was a light rain, so I kept the top up. "Wouldn't it be ironic," I said to Sara, "if I got busted for driving without a license on my way to see my grandfather in prison?"

Sara smiled a soft, sad smile. She was still weak but had really wanted to come along. I loved driving down the highway with her beside me. Part of me wished we could just keep driving and driving — go anywhere we wanted, stay anywhere we pleased.

At the prison, we were searched and scanned. The guards were cold and suspicious, and Sara was upset by how creepy it all was. I wondered if I'd made a mistake bringing her while she was still recovering from chemo. But once we were inside the prison, we were directed to go into a windowless room with a table and four chairs. I heard the door lock behind us, and shortly after, my grandfather walked in. I almost didn't recognize him. An old man with a short white beard, gray, thinning hair, old-style wire-rimmed glasses and fiery eyes.

"Trevor. God, it's good to see you." He leaned over and gave me a hug.

"This is Sara," I said.

He just looked at her and smiled. "Thanks for coming, both of you."

We sat down at the table, with Grandpop across from Sara and me.

"So they are releasing you? What happened?"

He sat back and took his glasses off. "Well, that's why I wanted you to come here, so I could tell you. It involves you."

"Me?" I asked.

Grandpop looked over at Sara and seemed cautious to proceed. "You know your mom called to tell me what that Dr. Duncan of yours said a while back," he began in a hesitating voice.

"Oh. Don't worry — Sara knows all about it."

He put his glasses back on. "I hope like hell it's not true. But after that she asked your doctor to write a letter to explain the situation for the parole hearing I had coming up." He stopped there and put his hands out, palms up.

"And?"

"And they granted me an early parole partly on compassionate grounds." He looked embarrassed. "I wanted you to hear it from me...in case you're pissed off or anything," he said.

For a second, it did make me feel strange. My convict grandfather was using my illness as a get-out-of-jail-free card. But instead of saying anything further about it, I reached across and took his hands. My grandfather squeezed my hands, and I suddenly realized how much we had missed out on.

Grandpop released my hands, then looked down at the table. "I've missed almost your whole life because of one stupid thing I did. And look what my actions did to your grandmother and your mother as well. It couldn't have been much worse. "

"But that's all over. You're getting out now."

"I should be happy, I know. But that mistake cost me so much." He looked at Sara again and then back at me. "You know, I did kill that guy. I was guilty."

I was shocked to hear him admit it out loud like that. I didn't know what to say.

"They called it manslaughter, and I guess it was, but I wanted you to hear the real story before I got out."

"You don't have to," I said.

"Yes, I do."

"Okay."

He took a deep breath. "Well, I was partners with this guy, Clive Jenkins, in a construction business. He was more of a businessman than I was, but I had the know-how when it came to building things. We mostly did small jobs — sheds and stairs and decks.

That sort of thing. I did the legwork, and he shuffled papers. I'd started thinking about going it on my own — could have made more money. And Clive — well, he was all talk. A good salesman and bullshitter, but he was dishonest. He didn't mind cheating customers out of money if he thought he could get away with it.

"So I had a couple of projects going on the side. Nothing big. But he found out. So he came over that day. I had been out in the garden with your grandmother, God rest her soul. We had gone inside, opened a bottle of wine and were playing cards. Then Clive showed up, driving this big old Caddie he had. He'd been drinking, and he started yelling at me in front of Joyce. Then he started pushing me — not hitting, just smacking my shoulder with his hand and calling me every name in the book. I'd always had a temper, but I was holding back. I wanted him to leave and told him so. But he kept pushing.

"And then Joyce walked up to him from behind and tried to pull him back. She was screaming for him to stop. That's when he hit her across the face — slapped her real hard. I guess I snapped then. I grabbed a shovel and hit him on the back of the head. Hit him hard. He went down and hit his head when he fell." My grandfather put his hands up in the air. "The jury found me guilty of manslaughter."

"It wasn't fair," I said. "They should have let you off."

"Well, the length of my sentence didn't seem fair to me or to your parents. But my reaction had been a violent one. And that was my mistake. I'd carried that anger and violence in me all my life, ever since I was a kid, and it finally came out."

"But you were defending yourself," Sara said. "And protecting your wife."

"Nonetheless, I'd lost control. Even in self-defense," he said, looking at me, "you should never let your brute instincts take over. I was guilty of that, and so here I am all these years later. God, I miss Joyce. And I wasn't there when she needed me. I wasn't even there when she passed on."

He took off his glasses and rubbed his eyes. "There. Those were the things I wanted to get off my chest. I wanted you to hear them before I got out."

"You going to come live at our house when you're released?"

"No way. I've brought enough grief on your family. I'll figure something out. I'm a cranky old man, Trevor, with some heavy baggage."

"But you're gonna need some help."

He nodded. "Well, I'll cross that bridge when I get to it. I got a little money saved from the life insurance after your grandmother died. Probably rent an apartment for starters. Figure it out from there."

"We've got some catching up to do," I said.

"Yes, indeed," he said.

The door he had come in through opened then. Time was up. He hugged me, and then he hugged Sara. "See you both real soon on the outside," he said as he turned to go.

TWENTY

I dropped Sara off at her home and then drove to the hotel. Instead of leaving the keys at the desk, I went up to Antonio's room and banged on the door. He answered, looking tired and disheveled. His room was a disaster zone.

"Let's go downstairs for a coffee," I said.

"Nah, I'm not really up for it."

Something wasn't right. This definitely was not the old Antonio. I insisted he come.

In the hotel restaurant, I told Antonio about my day, about my grandfather and his story.

"Life sucks," he said. "It doesn't make any sense. People don't make sense. Maybe coming back here wasn't such a good idea. It forces me to try to connect the dots that are the events of my life. And it doesn't all fit together. I feel like I've just been treading water, wasting my time."

"Then change it," I said.

"Some things you can't change," he said. "You should know that better than anyone."

"Fuck you," I said. I spit the words out before I could stop myself. I don't know exactly why, but he'd really pissed me off saying that. If I'd had a shovel, I think I might have smacked him.

"Yeah, fuck me. I already am fucked. The whole world is fucked."

"Maybe I can't change my situation. I'll live with that. But you can. Stop treading water and swim."

Antonio seemed at a loss for words. We sat silently for a minute, sipping our coffee as it got cold. "It's hard to explain," he finally said.

I backed off after that. We made small talk, and Antonio told me again he'd be leaving soon.

"We'll talk again before I go, old buddy," he said. "And listen, don't worry about me. You got your hands full."

But we never had that talk. Two days later, Antonio was driving on a highway outside of town — driving way too fast and way too crazy, is my guess. The story on the news said he was passing a tractor-trailer and found himself on a head-on collision course with a school bus filled with elementary school kids. Apparently, he steered the Porsche off the road to avoid a crash and slammed into a tree.

I was devastated by the news and haunted by my final conversation with my old friend. Haunted enough that I went back to the hotel to see if Antonio had left any message for me. But there was nothing. I also asked the manager if there was anything left in Antonio's room that seemed unusual.

"The place was a pigsty, but I've seen worse," the man said. "No, nothing really unusual."

So the story was that there was no story. Just a reckless young guy who'd gotten away with everything all his life. All except for this.

My parents were more worried about me than ever. Antonio's death made me think about my own inevitable ending. I felt certain about some of those symptoms now: memory problems, tightness along my spine, sudden movements of my fingers and arm.

Sara, however, was doing better day by day. After more blood tests, her doctor said he could see improvement. The chemo had destroyed most but not all of the cancer cells. She'd need some follow-up chemo, but nothing as heavy as before.

"I'm thinking about starting back to school," she told me one afternoon.

I'd been in a dark place in my mind ever since Antonio's death. Her words reflected the fact that she was getting better. I should have been happy. But instead, I had the sensation of being abandoned. "Great," I said.

"Maybe you should think about it too. What could it hurt?"

"Nothing, I guess." But I couldn't see myself walking through those doors again. Suddenly my future seemed a whole lot bleaker. I felt like Sara was slipping away.

"You know, even if I'm cancer-free after this, it can come back. So we need to get on with our lives."

"But who needs school?"

"I do. After going through all this, I just want to be as close to normal as possible. And I'm starting to think again about what I might do after high school. But I still need you, Trevor, more than anything. Everything changed for me once you came into the picture."

"And you…you changed my life. You changed me." I was looking into her beautiful eyes now. I was afraid something would happen and she would slip away. "But losing Antonio makes me think about how quickly things can change. How easily it can all disappear."

"That's why we have to live for now. We can't put things off. What was it Plank said?"

"He said to stop trying to figure it out."

"Have you thought any more about us?" she asked.

"Us?"

"Us. You know. Making love. Me getting pregnant maybe."

I shook my head. "I've thought about the making-love part. Thought about it a lot. But not the baby. It wouldn't be right."

Sara smiled the sweetest smile and reached out to touch my face. "I know. That was a fantasy on my part, I guess. But it felt good when I said it out loud."

###

A few days after that, I talked to Plank about an idea I had. I told him my grandfather was getting out of prison and needed a place to live. "He has money, so he could pay you rent. Maybe he could keep an eye on you, take care of some things around here."

Plank frowned. "An ex-con move in with me? What would the neighbors think?"

I could play his game. "Do you care what the neighbors think?"

"Hell no."

"Well, would you be willing to give it a try?"

"Let me think about it," he said. "I can see it now, two old geezers fighting over the TV remote and arguing about the dirty socks left on the floor." His voice was gruff, but I could tell he was struggling not to smile.

We had a party for Grandpop at my house when he got out, and then my dad drove him to Plank's house. The two of them didn't hit it off right away. Plank was crotchety and set in his ways, and my grandfather had spent all that time in prison, watching out for himself and scraping the scabs off old wounds. At first I thought it wasn't going to work out. But they must have had some kind of blow-up argument that cleared the air, because things started to settle down after that. They even started to find some common ground. Both of them had lost their wives along the way, and they both had regrets about their lives. They must have had some truly sad and dark conversations, which I think helped them to bond. And now I had a grandfather to visit along with getting Plank's signature no-bullshit advice when I needed it.

Sara's dad and I became friends of sorts. Sometimes when I showed up, Sara would be taking a nap — she was still tired a lot, but she seemed to be getting healthier. I talked to her dad about Antonio, and he listened. His marriage had broken up a long time back, and he'd been left alone to raise Sara. Like my dad, he blamed himself for his daughter being sick. I didn't think feeling guilty about things like that did anybody any good. Of course he was willing to go along with whatever Sara wanted. I thought she must even have told him she wanted to have sex with me. I didn't know that for certain, but he kept saying things like, "Make sure you treat my daughter with respect, whatever you do," and "Don't rush into something you're not ready for."

He may not have actually approved, but he did sometimes find reasons to leave the house when Sara and I were hanging out.

Sara and I had sex in her bedroom the afternoon before we both went back to school. We used a condom, which turned out to be more complicated than I expected. We were both shy at first. Having been through so much together, you would think it would have been easy and natural. I'm not sure what we were scared of. Once it was over, we both felt awkward and shy again. But we held each other tightly and looked into each other's eyes and knew it wouldn't be the last time we'd be together like this.

I was gently touching the top of Sara's head when I realized her hair was starting to grow back. "It tickles," she said and began to laugh.

So there we were the next day, like two seemingly normal teenage kids, standing in front of the high school. My high school. Sara had enrolled there after insisting she did not want to go back to Brookfield.

Sara was wearing her wig — the not-so-sexy one. I hadn't been seriously in school for a long time.

And I still wouldn't have been there if it wasn't for Sara. A few kids were friendly to me. Some were acquaintances who went as far back as my childhood days.

"Too bad about crazy old Antonio," a guy named Jason said, smiling like it was some kind of joke.

Brian, one of those jock types who always had something cruel to say to people, stopped when he saw me walking down the hall. "Trevor Marshall. Man, I thought you were dead." I gave him the finger and plotted some secret form of revenge. (*What would Antonio do?*)

After that, I can't say much of anything memorable happened. It was like I'd picked right up where I'd left off when I stopped going to school. Once my fear and anxiety began to wear off, it was, well, school. I was back in the world of the living. And it was rather boring.

A few weeks in, I met up with Sara as usual in the school cafeteria at lunchtime. It was noisy, and the kids were obnoxious. We were sitting off by the windows, away from the crowded tables, when Sara spotted her. A girl, maybe a little younger than us — a kind of plain-looking girl with a not-so-great complexion. She was all by herself at one end of a table with a crowd of loud, laughing girls at the other. She was wearing a scarf on her head. It was unmistakable.

Sara tapped me on the shoulder. "Let's go."

We went over to where the girl was and set our trays down across the table from her. "Okay if we sit here?" Sara asked.

The girl barely looked up, but she nodded.

As we settled down, we realized how many eyes were on us. What was the big deal? But it seemed to garner a lot of attention. And Sara knew we were being watched.

She cleared her throat loudly to catch the girl's attention. When the girl looked up, Sara said, "Watch this."

Slowly and dramatically, she pulled her wig off from front to back, held her head high and rubbed a hand over her beautiful, mostly bald head.

The girl was shocked at first. And then she smiled. While Sara still had the audience she wanted, she turned to me, took my face in her hands and kissed me hard on the lips.

It was safe to say we didn't go unnoticed that day.

EPILOGUE

Six months have gone by since that day in the cafeteria. You might be wondering about a lot of things.

Let's start with the list of what I wanted to do before I died.

1. Get drunk. (Seems pretty pointless now.)
2. Get stoned. (Never did get around to it.)
3. Drive a Lamborghini. (Fast cars are bad news in my book now.)
4. Get arrested. (I hear enough about life behind bars from the stories my grandfather tells me.)

5. Have a real girlfriend. (This turned out to be the only one that made any sense.)

And I guess you deserve an update on the list of things I wasn't going to tell you about, so here it is.

Too many details about where I live. (You still don't know much on that one.)

Why I love old, bad science-fiction movies. (I've mostly given them up. Girlfriends require attention — listen up, men.)

Most of my stupid, insane dreams — especially the ones involving monsters and girls in bikinis. (The monsters are all gone, and who needs fantasy girls these days?)

My hopes and aspirations and especially my never-to-be-fulfilled dream of being a marine biologist. Well, marine biologist and lawyer. (I don't think about a career anymore. I live one day at a time, and I keep my feet rooted in the present. And I didn't have to become a lawyer to help release my grandfather from jail. My HD did that. Go figure.)

My first three girlfriends — well, I thought of them as girlfriends, but they were really just friends or girls I wanted to be my girlfriend. (Friends are one thing; lovers are something entirely different.)

My problems, and there are several, mostly dull and obvious. (I still have problems. They didn't go away. But they don't rule my life.)

My philosophy of life. (I think you can figure that one out. Plank was a big help on that front, and so was Sara.)

How much money I have in the bank—all $1,278.80—saved over the course of a lifetime, mostly birthday money. (Well, that changed. Antonio had put me in his will. I was shocked when the lawyers called. I won't tell you how much, but it's a hell of a lot more than $1,278.80. But every time I think about the money, I feel sad. I grieve the loss of a really good friend.)

Most of my family history—except perhaps some details about my grandfather, who is currently in prison for a crime he committed a decade ago. (Grandpop is out, of course, and he and Plank are still living together. "The Odd Couple," Plank calls them. They argue like crazy but seem to enjoy it.)

My health issues — they say I have a year to live. Could be more, could be less. (I have symptoms that suggest the Huntington's is progressing, but I'm not down for the count yet. I have, as they say, something to live for, and I live it every day.)

As for now, I really don't have a list anymore —*any* fixed list — of the things I want to do before I die. I don't feel sorry for myself, and I wouldn't change anything. Well, if I could bring Antonio back, I would. If I could have prevented my grandfather from accidentally killing a man and going to prison, I would have changed that. But me and the Huntington's? Sure, I'd like to be healthy. But think about it. If I had not been in the hospital for blood tests, I would never have met Sara.

So let me leave you with this. Today at sunset, Sara and I stood on the top of that cliff by the sea. The gulls were flying above the waves. The sky had a mix of clouds over the sunset, but coppery blasts of light were shining in our eyes, and the wind was gently blowing through our hair. Sara and I had made it this far on our journey. Neither of us knew how much longer it was going to last.

And I guess that's where part two of Plank's Law comes into the picture. Imagination. Sara and I are both plenty smart, but we're just beginning to see the possibilities of what we might do with whatever time is left to us. We'll never be normal, and we'll just have to work with that. We'll live our lives minute by minute, make up our own set of rules or decide we don't want any rules at all. We'll write our own story together.

And whatever story that is, I know for damn sure it isn't going to be boring.

Lesley Choyce is the author of over ninety books of literary fiction, short stories, poetry, creative non fiction and young adult novels. He runs Pottersfield Press and has worked as editor with a wide range of Canadian authors. Choyce teaches Creative Writing at Dalhousie and he has won The Dartmouth Book Award, The Atlantic Poetry Prize and The Ann Connor Brimer Award. He has also been shortlisted for the Stephen Leacock Medal, The White Pine Award, The Hackmatack Award, The Canadian Science Fiction and Fantasy Award and, most recently, The Governor General's Literary Award. He was a founding member of the 1990s spoken-word rock band, The SurfPoets. He surfs year round in the North Atlantic. Lesley lives at Lawrencetown Beach, Nova Scotia. For more information, visit www.lesleychoyce.com.

More <u>BOLD</u> YA from ORCA